Wheels of fire

Robert Rigby

About the author

Robert Rigby is best known for writing the bestselling *Boy Soldier* series with Andy McNab. He began his career as a journalist, then turned to writing for radio, television and the theatre and has also directed and performed in children's theatre throughout the country. He wrote the novelizations of the movies, *Goal!* and *Goal II*, and a third novel in the series, *Goal: Glory Days*. His scripts for television include the long-running BBC children's drama, *Byker Grove*.

ALSO IN THIS SERIES

Running in her shadow

Parallel lines

Deep waters

Wheels of fire

An official
London 2012 novel

Robert Rigby

CARLTON
BOOKS

First published by Carlton Books Limited 2011
Copyright © 2011 Carlton Books Limited

London 2012 emblems: ™ & ® The London Organising Committee
of the Olympic Games and Paralympic Games Ltd (LOCOG) 2007.
London 2012 Pictograms © LOCOG 2009. All rights reserved.

Carlton Books Limited, 20 Mortimer Street, London, W1T 3JW.

A CIP catalogue record for this book is available from the British Library.

10 9 8 7 6 5 4 3 2 1

ISBN: 978-1-84732-813-7

Printed in the UK by CPI Mackays, Chatham, ME5 8TD

FSC
MIX
Paper
FSC® C020471

One

The two boys sat perched on the saddles of their BMX bikes, feet planted firmly on the ground. They were going nowhere, just waiting and watching. Through narrowed eyes, they scanned the roads and pavements, searching for their target.

On Saturday mornings, the town centre was at its busiest. Shoppers laden with heavy bags spilled from the mall, making their way towards bus stops and car parks.

Both boys were aged around fourteen. One of them, baseball cap swivelled round, picked anxiously at the rubber grips on his bike's handlebars as his eyes darted here and there. The other boy sat tall on his saddle, his arms crossed and an impatient, bad-tempered look plastered across his face.

'I hope I'm not wasting my time here, Jackie Boy,' he growled.

'You're not, T. Honest,' Jackie replied nervously. 'He always rides this way on Satur—' He stopped as he spotted the other biker's blazing eyes glaring in his direction.

'Who said you could call me T?'

'I... I... Everyone else...'

'*I'll* tell you when you can call me T. Till then, it's Travis. You got that?'

Jackie nodded. 'I got it. Sorry ... Travis.'

'And don't forget it.'

'No, I won't. I'm sorr— *There he is!*' Jackie's finger jabbed towards a younger boy who was slowly pedalling a BMX bike through the traffic.

'Him?' Travis asked. 'That's him?'

'That's Rory Temu. He's a legend, honest.'

'Doesn't look much of a legend. Just a scrawny kid.'

'But he's so fast.'

Travis laughed as he watched the young boy glance back before carefully passing a parked car. 'I reckon my granny could beat him.'

'I've seen him. Jumps, tricks—'

'We'll find out,' Travis interrupted. 'And you'd better be right.'

Jackie and Travis pushed away from the kerbside and rode after the boy, deliberately keeping their distance and making sure that, for the moment, he had no idea he was being followed.

The traffic gradually thinned as they cycled through quieter, narrow streets. Soon they were riding alongside a long wall and approaching a pair of tall, iron gates that marked the main entrance to a park. They watched Rory Temu cycle through the gates.

'See? He goes through the park, like I said,' Jackie muttered to Travis.

Travis nodded. 'Now we'll let him know we're here.'

The two boys began pedalling harder.

'Hey, Temu!' Travis shouted as they hurtled after him.

The young boy looked back, his face registering surprise as he spotted the two riders approaching quickly.

'I want you!' Travis yelled.

Rory seemed to hesitate for a moment, as if he was deciding what to do. Then he turned away and sped off, his feet driving hard on the pedals.

But the older boys were already travelling at high speed and closing on him rapidly.

'I thought you said he was fast!' Travis yelled to Jackie as he surged forward. 'I'll have him off that wreck he's riding, no bother.'

Travis left Jackie trailing. As he closed on Rory, he let go of the bike's handlebars with his right hand. He came alongside Rory and drew back his arm, a cruel grin on his face.

But as Travis's hand swept forward to knock him from his bike, Rory suddenly spurted ahead and the older boy connected with nothing but fresh air. Unbalanced, his bike wobbled dangerously, out of control. Travis frantically grabbed the handlebars, just managing to stop his BMX from crashing to the ground. His face was red with rage.

'You little—!' Furiously, he tried to catch up.

But Rory Temu was moving like lightning now and Travis was losing even more ground. It was obvious that he was never going to catch up.

'Wait!' he shouted. 'Look, I only want to talk!'

As the young rider increased the distance between them, his reply could only just be heard. 'Yeah, of course you do.'

Rory swerved off the main tarmac walkway onto a narrower mud track that wound its way through a wooded area. He hardly slowed, flinging his bike one way and then the other, leaving his pursuers further behind with every turn of the pedals.

But Travis kept up the chase, following doggedly as Rory rode back onto the main path and sped towards a small gate that led from the park onto a quiet street. Although the exit was open, there was an iron bollard in the middle. A person could walk around it easily, but there was no way a cyclist or a skateboarder could speed through. If they didn't dismount or at least slow down, they'd cannon right into the bollard. 'Stop...' Travis's voice trailed away.

Rory wasn't even slowing.

Travis stared. The young rider was going to smash into the iron bollard. He couldn't get through, not at that speed.

But he did.

With a double flick of his wrists and a twitch of the handlebars, Rory jinked his body and bike twice to avoid the bollard and somehow squeeze through an impossibly narrow gap on one side.

Travis gasped in amazement, bringing his own bike to a skidding standstill long before reaching the bollard. 'Legend,' he breathed, with a shake of his head. He was still staring at the exit and trying to work out *how* the young rider had managed to get himself and his bike through without a scratch when Jackie arrived a few seconds later.

'See? See what I mean?' the other boy said breathlessly.

Travis nodded slowly. 'You've done well, Jackie Boy. Really well.'

'I knew you'd like him.'

'Oh, I like him all right.' As he turned to Jackie, Travis's smile was almost as menacing as his scowl. 'And you can call me T.'

Two

Rory wasn't worried about the high-speed chase. Things like that happened in his part of the city.

He lived in Edinburgh, on the northern side of the Scottish capital and far from the tourist sights and the expensive shopping streets. It was a tough area, but Rory had been born and brought up there, quickly learning to look after himself. He was streetwise and the occasional bit of trouble didn't bother him too much.

But right now he was puzzled. As he wheeled his BMX into the yard at the back of his house, he was still trying to figure out why the two boys had chased him.

He undid the combination lock on the shed door and pushed his bike carefully inside. The bike was old and battered and had seen much better days, but Rory loved it. He felt that it was almost part of him.

'Maybe they wanted my bike?' he said to himself, locking up the shed and checking more closely than usual that the lock was properly fixed. 'No way.'

He went into the house through the back door. His

mum, Mary, was cooking at the ancient kitchen stove.

'All right, Mum?' Rory asked, squeezing past and sitting down on one of three mismatched and slightly rocky chairs clustered around the kitchen table.

Mary nodded. 'How were your nan and grandad?'

'Cool,' Rory answered.

'And what about your mum?' Mary said, lifting a large pan over to the sink. 'Is she cool, too?'

Rory watched the steam rise as his mum carefully drained rice into a colander.

'Super cool,' he said.

Mary smiled. 'That's me. Call your sister, will you?'

Rory got up and walked towards the hallway.

'Shoes,' his mum said, without even looking in Rory's direction.

Rory grinned and kicked off his trainers. 'Super cool,' he said as he went upstairs.

Most Saturdays, when Rory got home and Grace had been dragged away from her books or the computer, Mary and her children sat down and had a meal together.

Mary worked every evening but Saturday, so she

really looked forward to her night off. And so did her kids, because she was a great cook.

'Wicked chicken, Mum,' Rory said, tucking into his dinner.

'I don't know how you do it,' Grace added.

'I'll show you,' Mary answered. 'It's easy.'

'No. I mean, how you afford it.'

'Mary shrugged. 'That's easy, too. There's amazing bargains in the reduced section just before the supermarket closes. All the best stuff at half the price.'

'I wish you'd let me get a Saturday job,' Grace said. 'Then I could help a bit.'

'You don't have time for a job,' said Mary. 'You have to study and pass your exams for university.'

Grace was sixteen and the brainy member of the family. She already had ten top GCSE passes and had started studying for four A levels.

'But, Mum—'

'Eat your chicken,' Mary said kindly. 'Your food will be cold after all this talking.'

'But—'

'Look, your brother's almost finished and you've hardly started.'

Rory had almost cleared his plate, but he wasn't anywhere near finished. He picked up a serving spoon and helped himself to another piece of chicken. 'I went to see Mr Malik at the paper shop today,' he said. 'I asked him if there were any paper rounds going.'

'You didn't tell me,' Mary said.

'I wanted to surprise you, if I got the job.'

'And did you?'

Rory shook his head. 'Mr Malik said that there aren't so many rounds now. He reckons that people don't buy papers any more, not like they used to. And anyway, I'm not allowed to do a round until I'm thirteen. That's months away.'

'I don't get it,' Mary said, pretending to be cross. 'Why are both my children so desperate to go out to work?' She looked at them sternly. 'There'll be plenty of time for you to work when you're older. And in the meantime, you don't need to worry. We can manage.'

'I'm not worried,' Rory said with a smile. 'I want a paper round so I can save for a new BMX. Mr Malik said that he'll try to sort me out when I am thirteen. I'm faster on the bike than anyone he's got working for him now, he says.'

Rory turned his attention back to the meal and they ate in silence for a couple of minutes.

But then Mary put down her knife and fork. 'Actually,' she said hesitantly, 'I've got a surprise for you.'

Rory and Grace stopped eating. Neither looked delighted to hear that there was a surprise in store, because both had an idea of what it might be.

'What is it, Mum?' Grace asked.

'It's a good surprise,' Mary said hurriedly, as though she was trying to convince herself as much as them.

Rory looked doubtful. 'Really?'

'Yes, really,' Mary said. She took a deep breath and then said softly, 'Your dad's coming home.'

Rory and Grace exchanged a brief look but said nothing.

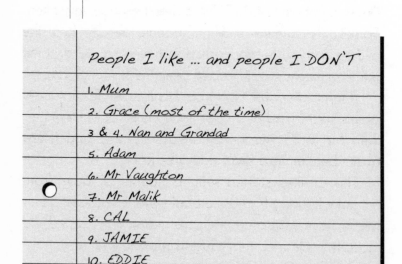

People I like ... and people I DON'T
1. Mum
2. Grace (most of the time)
3 & 4. Nan and Grandad
5. Adam
6. Mr Vaughton
7. Mr Malik
8. CAL
9. JAMIE
10. EDDIE

Rory liked making lists. He'd done it for years. He made all sorts of lists: people, places, BMX tricks, sports, food, music. Almost anything could be ranked from one to ten.

At the top of each list, numbers one to three were the people or things he liked the most. They were followed by more likes, all the way down to number seven. But the last three numbers, always written in capitals, were the dislikes. Number ten was the very worst place to be.

Rory lay stretched out on his bed later that Saturday evening, chewing his pen as he looked at his 'People I like and people I DON'T' list. It didn't change very often. Sometimes a new friend might come and go from the middle section, but the top spots never altered and the name at the very bottom had been the same for years.

Rory studied the list again. His family was followed by his best friend at school, then his favourite teacher, then Mr Malik, who was always friendly and joked about becoming a BMX rider like Rory.

The dislikes started with a couple of boys from school who Rory had done battle with in the past. Then finally, at number ten, was the name Rory hated the most. It made him angry just to read it.

EDDIE.

Rory underlined Eddie's name. 'If I had a longer list, you'd be at the bottom of that, too,' he muttered. '*Dad.*'

Three

Rory was deep in thought. It was Monday, which meant that there were five long days at school to get through before he would be free again. But Rory wasn't thinking of the countless lessons he'd have to endure before the weekend. He had other things on his mind.

Usually, English with Mr Vaughton was Rory's favourite subject at school. At least, it occupied the number-one spot on his 'Subjects I like ... and subjects I DON'T' list right now. This was mainly because, as far as Rory was concerned, Mr Vaughton was just about the only teacher in the entire school who made lessons interesting.

Usually, but not today. The lesson had only just begun, but Rory's thoughts had already drifted away. One thing loomed large in his mind – and it wasn't English. He'd felt troubled from the moment his mum had revealed that his dad was 'coming home'.

'Coming home' meant that Eddie Temu was being released from prison. Rory hadn't bothered keeping track of how long his dad had been away this time. It had happened so many times now that Eddie seemed to have been in prison for longer than he'd been out of it.

Eddie Temu was a thief, and despite their mum telling them on Saturday that he was really a good man who deserved another chance, both Rory and Grace believed that he would always be a thief.

Every time that Eddie was about to be released from prison, he somehow managed to convince Mary that he had changed. And each time that he arrived home, he told them all, very sincerely, that this time it would be different.

For a few weeks, he would sit around the house, scrounging money from Mary and telling his family that he was looking for a job. But he never seemed to find work, or if he did, it only lasted for a day or two. Then a few weeks later, he would be arrested again, and soon after that, he would be back in prison.

It didn't really bother Rory when his dad went back to jail; Eddie deserved it. But it did bother Rory how it affected his mum. Every time, she was devastated all over again. Rory hated seeing her tears as his dad was taken away, and there were always more tears in the weeks that followed.

This was why Rory hated his dad and dreaded him coming home. He stared out of the classroom window, imagining the big, false smile and the hug Eddie would give him when he first got back.

'So what do you think, Rory?'

Rory didn't hear the teacher's voice; his thoughts were locked onto his dad. Then he felt an elbow dig gently into his ribs. He turned to see Adam staring at him. His best friend nodded towards the front of the classroom. Rory suddenly realized where he was, and that many pairs of eyes were staring in his direction. Then he noticed Mr Vaughton smiling at him, waiting for the response to his question.

But Rory had no idea what his teacher had been talking about.

'Sorry, sir?'

'I wanted to know what you think.'

'Er … think about what?'

'London 2012?'

Rory's mind was blank. 'London what?'

All around the room there were groans and sighs as Rory's classmates shook their heads or raised their eyes to the ceiling.

Jamie Finter – who was way down at number nine on Rory's people list – was quick to comment. 'I don't think Rory's with us today, sir. He's riding his BMX in dreamland.'

A ripple of laughter spread around the classroom.

'All right,' Mr Vaughton said. 'Thank you, Jamie. I

always said you should be a comedian.'

There was more laughter.

Mr Vaughton was the only teacher at the school who wasn't from Scotland. He was English – from Yorkshire – and very popular, not least because of the way he played up the sporting rivalry between Scotland and England. Every time an international rugby or football match drew near, the light-hearted banter between teacher and pupils would kick off and continue until long after the game had been played.

'Settle down, please. Even you, Jamie,' Mr Vaughton said, before turning back to Rory. 'Well, if I can't interest you, maybe the film will.'

'Sorry, sir,' Rory said. 'I was thinking about—'

'Never mind. Let's just watch the film.'

But there was another interruption.

Jamie's hand shot up. 'Sir!'

'Yes, what is it?' Mr Vaughton said patiently.

'London 2012 is all about England. We should be seeing a film about Scotland.'

Mr Vaughton was used to Jamie's attempts to wind him up. 'London 2012 is about the whole of Great Britain, and the whole world,' he said. 'And don't forget, all the home-nation countries – Scotland, England, Wales and Northern Ireland – compete as Team GB.'

'But Scotland has the best cyclist, sir,' Jamie said.

Mr Vaughton frowned, as though he didn't know who Jamie was talking about. 'Oh, and who might that be?'

Thirty voices shouted out the answer. 'Chris Hoy!'

'Oh, yes,' Mr Vaughton teased. 'Well, I suppose he's not bad, and he's from Edinburgh, too.'

Everyone was proud of the great cyclist, who'd won gold many times over. If everything went to plan, he would be on the hunt for more glory at London 2012.

'Actually,' Mr Vaughton said, 'Sir Chris started out racing BMX when he was a lad. He was one of the best in the world.' He looked over at Rory. 'Did you know that?'

Rory shook his head. 'No, sir.'

'Right, let's watch the film,' Mr Vaughton said. 'I'm sure it'll inspire you for the next stage of your London 2012 projects, much better than I can.' He glanced at Rory once more as he spoke.

The opening music to the film began and Rory silently told himself to stop thinking about his dad. He'd wasted too much time on him already.

The film started by showing how run-down areas and waste ground on the eastern edge of London had been transformed into beautiful parkland. Then the towering Olympic Stadium, the amazing Aquatics Centre and the Cycling VeloPark – with its Velodrome and fantastic BMX track – came into view.

'Not like round here, is it?' Jamie said loudly.

'Shhhh!' said at least ten voices.

Rory leaned forward, his eyes widening as the cycling venues filled the screen.

'Rory's wide awake at last, sir!' Jamie called. 'He's imagining riding round the Velodrome with Sir Chris.'

'I'm delighted for him,' Mr Vaughton replied. 'And I'd be even more happy if you could manage to keep quiet.'

Rory didn't hear their voices or the fresh peal of laughter that followed Mr Vaughton's comments. His thoughts were elsewhere again. And for once, Jamie had been almost correct with his jokey comment. But it wasn't the Velodrome that Rory was daydreaming about and in his imagination he was alone.

As the incredible London 2012 BMX track appeared on the television screen, Rory could see himself riding it. Bursting from the starting gate, sliding round the corners, hurtling down the straights, rocketing into the bumps and flying through the air, wheels spinning, heart racing.

He could almost feel every bruising bump and twisting turn and the surge of blistering speed and power as his BMX hurtled over the finish line. It felt amazing.

If only he could ride there for real.

Four

They seemed to appear out of nowhere; Rory didn't even see them coming. One moment he was riding slowly along, thinking to himself that the London 2012 site had gone straight to number one on his list of places to see, the next he'd been forced to come to a standstill, completely surrounded by boys on bikes.

There were five of them, their front wheels pointing towards Rory, back wheels sticking outwards, like the points of a star. Rory was imprisoned in the middle, wondering what was going on.

He didn't recognize any of the boys. They looked older than him by a year or two, but not one of the faces was familiar. And for the moment, no one seemed in any hurry to put a name to his face. They were all just staring.

Rory instantly saw that there was no easy escape. But his mind was working quickly, trying to figure out what his best move would be if he had to make a sudden break for freedom.

He stared bravely at the boy directly in front of him. 'What d'you want?'

There was a hint of menace in the boy's quiet reply. 'Don't remember me, do you, Rory?'

Rory shook his head slowly. But inside he was thinking hard. If the boy knew his name, it meant that this wasn't just a chance meeting. So what did they want?

'I'm Travis.'

Rory shrugged. The name meant nothing to him.

'Last Saturday,' Travis said, 'me and Jackie Boy followed you through the park.'

'Oh, that,' Rory said, remembering the high-speed pursuit. 'Chased me, you mean.'

'Chased, followed,' Travis said. 'Doesn't matter.'

'It matters to me when I don't even know you,' Rory said. 'What was it all about?'

Travis smiled. 'I wanted to see if you're as good on that bike as Jackie Boy said. And you are. No, scratch that. You're even better than he said. I've still got no idea how you got through that gap.'

'Magic,' Rory said bravely. 'I can do loads of tricks.'

'I've heard,' Travis answered.

Rory turned his bike's front wheel slightly to the left and edged forward a little. 'So, I got away from you and now you want to do something about it.' He glared at each of the boys in turn. 'And it takes five of you? Oh, I'm really scared.'

Travis laughed. 'Very brave, Rory. That's good, 'cos you need to be brave to be one of us.'

'One of you?' said Rory. 'What are you talking about?'

'I want you to join my team,' Travis said. He grinned as he saw the look of confusion on Rory's face. 'All five of us are fast on bikes,' he continued. 'But none of us can keep up with you, not even Craig here.' He gestured towards the boy on his left. 'And we all thought he was the fastest around.'

From the moment the gang had ridden up, Craig had been glaring at Rory as though he'd like to thump him. But now his glare turned to a look of pure hatred. His eyes bored into Rory's. 'You don't know that he's faster than me, T,' he said coldly, not shifting his gaze. 'He's just a kid. I could take him, easy.'

Travis laughed. 'That's what I thought, Craig. But he's good, very good. I reckon he'd beat you.'

'Well, let's find out right now,' Craig snapped angrily.

'Later,' Travis said. He turned back to Rory. 'So, are you gonna join us?'

'Doing what?' Rory said, still feeling confused. 'Racing, is that what you mean?'

All five boys, even the furious Craig, started to laugh.

And Rory didn't like the sound of their laughter.

'So, come on then,' he said. 'What is it you do?'

Travis lifted one hand from his handlebars, silencing the others. 'Well, Rory,' he said, grinning, 'what we do is … steal things.'

Rory said nothing.

'Bikes mainly,' Travis went on, as though stealing were perfectly normal. 'But other things, too. And then we sell them. We make good money and you'd get plenty. You'd like that, eh, Rory?'

When he didn't reply, Travis continued. 'Someone as fast as you would be great for us. What d'you reckon, then?'

Five pairs of eyes stared at Rory as the boys waited for his decision. For an instant, he found himself thinking that having the money would mean he could help his mum out *and* afford a new bike. And then he remembered his dad, and the shame he'd brought on his family. One thief in the family was more than enough.

'No, I'm not in,' Rory said quietly. 'I don't want to know. Now get out my way – I'm going.'

For a few tense seconds, no one moved and Rory could almost hear his heart thumping in his chest. But then Travis nodded to the boy sitting on his right.

'Let him out, Jackie Boy.'

Slowly, the boy eased his bike back, allowing Rory

to edge his BMX through the gap.

As soon as he was clear, Rory's feet quickly found the pedals and he rode swiftly away, making ground as fast as he could, just in case the gang decided to give chase.

But Travis was smiling as he watched the young boy speed away. 'Look after yourself, Rory!' he shouted. 'I'll be seeing you very soon!'

Five

Rory and Grace were staring impatiently at the computer in her bedroom. They were trying to get onto a website and it was taking ages.

Grace sighed. 'This old thing is so, so slow. It drives me crazy when I'm researching stuff.'

Rory wasn't that interested in computers. All he wanted was to check out the website Mr Vaughton had recommended. There were some BMX video clips on there and he really wanted to see them.

'Why is it so slow?' he asked.

'Because it's ancient and worn out, and it wasn't very good to start with, and I need a new one.' Grace turned away from the screen and looked at her brother. 'But new computers cost mega money, so I can't see us getting one for a long time, can you?'

Rory didn't answer because Travis's words had flashed into his mind. *We make good money and you'd get plenty.*

With money, Rory would be able to help his sister

and his mum. And the way Travis had spoken made it sound so easy. But Rory felt sick at even the thought of stealing. He wasn't going to get involved, no chance.

'And with Dad coming home,' Grace continued, 'we'll probably have even less money. You know what he's like. We'll both have to look out for Mum.'

Rory nodded. 'When will he be back?' he asked, fearing the answer would be 'very soon'.

'Mum's not sure. A couple of weeks, maybe?'

The website had finally loaded. 'At last!' Grace clicked on the link for videos and the waiting began again. 'I hope this is worth it. I'm supposed to be doing maths.'

'I know,' Rory said. 'But Mr Vaughton wanted me to see this stuff. He said that it might inspire me.'

Grace raised her eyebrows. 'It's about time you were inspired by something, or someone.'

'Just get it on the screen, eh?' said Rory. 'You'll love it.'

'Yeah. Sure I will.'

'It's clips of our top BMX riders.'

'How exciting,' Grace teased. 'So is that what you suddenly want to do? Be a BMX rider? Compete at the Olympic Games?'

Rory shrugged his shoulders and thought for a moment. 'I don't know. Maybe I could if I really wanted to and I worked really hard. Not London 2012, but maybe the Games after that.' He nodded at the screen. 'We're in.' The video link had finally opened.

Grace folded her arms and sat back to watch.

'I want to see Shanaze Reade and Liam Phillips,' Rory said. 'Shanaze's been world champion three times. And she was in the last Olympics in Beijing.'

Grace looked impressed. 'How do you know all this? You're never usually this clued-up.'

'Mr Vaughton told me. He's in a bike club,' Rory said. 'He knows loads of stuff about bike racing.'

'Mr Vaughton? Really?'

Rory nodded, his eyes fixed on the video. 'Shh. Just watch.'

Brother and sister sat close together, watching Shanaze Reade line up with the other riders at the start of one of her world-championship-winning races. And from the moment the starting gate went down, it was obvious that Shanaze was totally determined to win. She hurtled towards the first crucial turn and then battled down the second straight.

'Isn't he a bit old for bike racing?' Grace said.

'What?' Rory replied, his eyes still glued to the computer screen. 'Who?'

'Mr Vaughton.'

'Oh.' Rory's eyes widened as he watched the tightly bunched BMX riders lean into a corner. 'He doesn't race now, but he used to do track and road racing.

He still rides a mountain bike. And he's met Sir Chris Hoy!'

On screen, Shanaze crossed the line to claim victory.

'Awesome!' Rory said, turning away from the screen at last. 'Liam Phillips now.'

Grace raised her eyebrows. 'Rory, I should be getting on with my maths.'

'Yeah, I know. But remember what mum keeps telling you?' Rory said quickly. 'You have to give that enormous brain of yours a break sometimes.'

'Very funny.'

'Go on, Grace...'

She hesitated for a moment. 'Oh, all right. But this is the last one.'

This time they watched in silence and when it was all over, Rory sat back in his chair, his thoughts racing even faster than a speeding BMX. 'Liam's already won two silver medals at the world championships,' he said. 'But now he's injured, so he'll switch to Track Cycling for London 2012. It's a really tough sport, you know.'

'Yeah, I think I've got the picture now,' Grace said, closing the website. 'You know all about BMX racing. And I'm impressed, but I really do need to do my maths. So, *out!*'

Her brother smiled, got up from the chair and walked towards the door.

'Rory?'

He stopped and looked back at his sister. 'Yeah?

'If you really want to do it, you should go for it.'

Rory nodded. 'I'd like to. Real racing on a proper BMX track would be so cool.'

'It'd be expensive though,' Grace added. 'Helmets and clothes... You'd maybe even need a new bike. That lot would cost more than you'd get from a paper round.'

Rory sighed. Money again. Everything always came back to money. 'I'll do it somehow,' he said. 'And if I'm rich and famous one day, do you know what else I'll do?'

'No,' Grace answered. 'What will you do?'

Rory grinned. 'I'll buy you a new computer.'

Six

Rory was concentrating hard as he sped along. Not only did he have to watch the track as it twisted and turned through the trees, he had to look out for bumps and hollows on the tricky course, too.

It was brilliant fun.

Rory was so glad that he'd taken Mr Vaughton's advice and entered one of the special *Pedal Through The Park* races organized by the local council. There were races for all age groups. Mr Vaughton had already taken part in the adult event and had managed a top-ten finish.

Now, it was Rory's turn. He was one of the youngest riders in the race for twelve- to fourteen-year-old boys. He knew that his BMX wasn't the best machine for the course. Mountain bikes with thicker tyres and more gears were better suited to the rough ground and most competitors rode those. But Rory wasn't thinking about the other riders' bikes as he pedalled furiously, his bike eating up the ground and closing on the boy in front.

The track was so narrow that there would never have been enough room for all twenty-five competitors to ride together, so the race was actually a time trial over two-and-a-half kilometres.

The riders set off at two-minute intervals and went three times round the winding, tricky circuit. Each rider was timed and the winner was the biker who completed the course in the fastest time.

Rory was edging closer and closer to the boy in front. Very few riders had actually overtaken, but it looked as though Rory, on his last lap, might do just that.

'Come on, Rory!'

Rory glanced to his left and grinned as he caught a fleeting glimpse of Mr Vaughton and Grace standing at the side of the track.

'You can do it!' Grace yelled. 'Remember Shanaze!'

Rory had almost reached the rear wheel of the boy in front as they went into the tightest turn on the course, wheels spinning, dust rising from the dry mud. He leaned into the bend, his right pedal close to the ground. Rory knew exactly what he was doing, and as he came out of the turn and straightened up, there was little more than a wheel's length between Rory's BMX and the other, older boy's mountain bike.

Spectators lined both sides of the long, final straight,

and a few began to cheer as the two boys powered into view. Suddenly, the time trial had turned into a proper race between two riders.

More and more spectators were cheering and shouting, the majority of them supporting the younger, smaller rider. The underdog. Rory.

'Go on, laddie!'

'You can do it!'

Rory was loving every second. This was fantastic – one-against-one, battling it out to the end.

He pedalled furiously, lifted himself out of the saddle and began his bid to pass the other rider. There was just room to get by, and Rory's face was set with determination as he edged his BMX alongside his rival's bike.

But the other rider obviously didn't like the idea of being overtaken. He glanced to his left and glared at the younger boy at his side, and then moved his bike closer, forcing Rory to swerve towards the side of the course and the rope boundary.

It was a dangerous manoeuvre. Spectators on the other side of the rope stepped back towards the line of trees.

'Look out!' someone shouted.

'Watch it!' another man yelled. 'You'll crash!'

Rory didn't flinch as the other bike came nearer and nearer, so close that they were almost touching. Then, with a sudden burst of speed, Rory swept forward, passing his rival and hurtling on towards the finish.

Cheers and applause rang out from the spectators clustered around the finish as Rory crossed the line three bike lengths ahead of the other boy. His grin stretched from ear to ear as he saw one of the race officials click his stopwatch.

Rory brought his bike to a standstill, smiling modestly. He didn't spot the five boys who stood a little further back from the main crowd. The boys had watched the powerful sprint finish very closely.

'Our Rory's done well, eh?' Travis said.

'He has, T,' one boy replied, while the others nodded.

Travis started to clap his hands. 'Come on, lads,' he said. 'Join in with everyone else.'

One by one the other boys started to applaud.

'That's right,' Travis said. 'We'll have to make absolutely certain Rory joins us now. Eh, lads?'

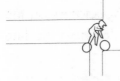

'And in third place, we have one of our youngest competitors and a first-time rider in the competition ... Rory Temu.'

Rory stepped forward self-consciously, embarrassed by the ringing applause. He walked over to the wooden podium and stepped onto it.

'Look out, Sir Chris!' a voice boomed. 'Rory's coming!' There was a smattering of laughter and Rory looked up to see Mr Vaughton beaming at him and giving a thumbs-up sign. Grace stood next to the teacher, smiling but looking almost as embarrassed as her younger brother.

A man wearing a chain of office stepped forward and slipped a ribbon around Rory's neck. The shiny medal lay heavily against his chest.

'Well done, laddie,' the mayor said, offering his hand for Rory to shake.

Rory was red-faced. He'd never won a medal before or shaken hands with anyone. Tentatively, he stretched out his right hand and waited. He didn't need to worry because the man shook it vigorously and then let go, before quickly moving on to the next medal-winner.

Rory held his medal. He'd come third in his first-ever race – he could hardly believe it. It felt good. Fantastic. And it made Rory want to win more medals.

When the presentations were over, he wandered over to where Mr Vaughton and Grace were chatting.

'Great ride, Rory,' Mr Vaughton said. 'I was just saying to Grace that if you were half as good in English as you are on that bike, you'd be a genius.'

'Thanks, sir.' Rory smiled. 'Not much chance of that.'

Mr Vaughton laughed. 'Listen, why don't you come along to my bike club and see if you fancy joining? There's a BMX section.'

Rory hesitated. 'I don't know, sir. Is it... Is it expensive?'

Mr Vaughton shook his head. 'It's completely free for under-fourteens.'

'Oh, right. Well, I ... I might be interested.'

'Rory, you'd love it. You know you would,' Grace said quickly. 'You were saying the other night how much you wanted to race on a proper BMX track.'

'I know, but—'

'Have a word with your mum,' Mr Vaughton said. 'If she's happy for you to give it a try, you can come down to the club and see how you get on.'

Rory nodded. 'Thanks. I will.'

'Right,' Mr Vaughton said. 'I'm off home. See you both at school.'

'Bye, sir,' Grace and Rory said together.

They collected Rory's bike and then strolled towards the park exit. Rory talked non-stop about the time trial, relating every detail he could remember, while his sister listened patiently.

And both of them were completely unaware of the five boys on bikes who were slowly and silently following.

Seven

It was turning out to be a great evening. Everyone was incredibly friendly and Rory was learning so much about BMX racing.

He was amazed at the sheer number of young riders who were enjoying trial runs on the track or milling around the sidelines. And what surprised Rory even more was that many of the riders – boys and girls – were much younger than him. Some looked as if they were no more than seven- or eight-years-old.

BMX racing was obviously a fast-growing sport. Rory had already decided that he definitely wanted to be part of it.

To start with, he rode the course a few times with other young newcomers. The cycling club's BMX coach, Phil Jacks, nodded his approval to Mr Vaughton. Together, they watched as Rory smoothly took the tight bends and rode the bumpy, dipping straights like a much more experienced racer – and a lot faster than the other newcomers.

'He's a natural,' Phil said to Mr Vaughton. 'He looks almost ready to race. Let's see how he manages the starting gate.' This was the mechanical gate that was used for proper races.

Phil gathered Rory and five other new boys together and asked them to ride up onto the gate. Its metal front was raised and the boys manoeuvred their bikes into the starting lanes behind.

'Right,' the coach said. 'We're going to practise a start. But before we do, let me remind you that once the gate goes down, you'll all be hurtling towards the bend to try to get around it first. Okay?'

All six riders nodded their agreement.

'Good,' Phil continued. 'But remember, this is not a fairground and you are not on the dodgems and the idea is *not* to knock as many other riders off their bikes as you can. Do that in a race and it's likely to be judged unsportsmanlike conduct and you'll be thrown out. Disqualified. Got it?'

Rory and the others grinned at each other and then nodded again.

'Right,' Phil said. 'So let's go through what happens at the start.'

He explained that the mechanical gate would drop after a series of recorded starting instructions that riders had to follow.

'It's like a running or swimming race, only our

jargon is a bit different,' Phil said with a smile. 'And it's maybe a bit more fun, too. Instead of, "On your marks, get set", we go for, "Okay, riders, let's set 'em up", and then, "Riders ready!" More exciting, eh?'

The new riders nodded enthusiastically. They were all raring to go.

'Then instead of a starting pistol,' Phil said, 'you get the third instruction, which is, "Watch the gate!" You've got to be ready to go then, because next you'll hear four beeps and the gate will drop, and then you're away. Right, let's give it a shot.'

The six boys got ready to make their first proper racing starts, manoeuvring their bikes to the front of the gate.

'Remember,' Phil told them, 'snap out of the gate as quickly as you can and try to get to the berm in the lead.'

One boy put up a hand. 'What's a "berm"?'

'It's our word for a banked corner. If you're in the lead after the first one, you've got a good chance of taking the best line round the rest of the track.' He clapped his hands twice. 'Okay, let's go for it.'

Another boy put up his hand. 'So, do we stop after we've made the start?'

'Well, you could,' Phil said, smiling. 'On the other hand, it's the end of the evening and we *could* make a race of it before we pack up for the night. What d'you reckon?'

'Race!' the new riders shouted together.

'Right, then. Race it is.'

Rory tried to stay calm. He was on his own bike, but wearing a full-face helmet and gloves that had been lent to him for the evening by the club. He felt like a proper racer and was desperate to do well. But he knew that it was important to stay cool and not get overexcited.

They all listened to the starting instructions and when the *Watch the gate!* command came, they all leaned forward on their pedals as the four beeps counted down. Then the gate fell and the six riders went hurtling forward. Rory was in one of the centre lanes at the start, but with the first few lightning-fast rotations of his pedals he moved speedily to the front of the pack.

There was no doubt that Rory would be first into the berm and he emerged from the corner with a clear lead.

From then on, no one got near him. The rest of the field could do no more than fight it out for second place.

'Wow, Richard,' Phil said to Mr Vaughton as they watched Rory turn into the final straight. 'It looks like you might have found us a new star.'

'I was pretty sure he'd be good,' the teacher replied.

Rory crossed the finish line more than fifteen metres ahead of the rider who trailed in second.

'In a way, it's a pity he won so easily,' Phil said. 'I would have liked to have seen him battle for it more.'

Mr Vaughton smiled. 'Oh, he'll battle when he needs to. I'm pretty sure about that as well.'

Eight

That night, Rory hardly slept. His first experience of real BMX racing had left him buzzing with excitement.

He lay in bed thinking over the events of the evening and wishing that he'd taken up the sport sooner. Becoming a serious BMX rider had gone straight to the top of his 'Things I want to do ... and things I DON'T' list.

Rory had never been especially interested in sport. He enjoyed playing football at school and was a decent midfielder. But it was just for fun. He didn't watch football. Hibernian, the Scottish Premier League team, played at their Easter Road stadium not far from where Rory lived, but he had never stepped inside the ground.

Even his BMX had been strictly for pleasure – not a proper sport. Mastering a new trick with which to impress his mates had been more fun than the idea of serious, high-speed racing. But all that had changed. Rory wanted to race, and he wanted to be the best.

As the clock ticked on and the minutes turned into hours, Rory lay there, knowing that his new plan would mean a lot of hard work and total dedication. But he was up for it. When he finally drifted off to sleep, his dreams were filled with fantastic races and Olympic Games glory.

After school the following day, Rory walked home wondering how he could scrape together the cash to buy a good helmet and proper gloves. He didn't get much in the way of pocket money and he found himself wishing once again that he were old enough to start that paper round Mr Malik had promised – or almost promised.

The route home took Rory close to the shopping precinct, and as he turned a corner he saw someone he recognized. It was one of the boys from the gang – the boy Travis had said was their fastest BMX rider.

But at that moment, the boy wasn't at all fast. He wasn't even slow. He was sitting on the pavement, rocking backward and forward with both arms clasped around his right leg, going nowhere.

Rory walked over to him, remembering that Travis

had called the boy Craig.

'You all right?'

Craig looked up, the same hostility Rory had spotted before burning in his eyes. 'Do I *look* all right?'

'What happened?'

'I fell, didn't I? Tripped. And I've hurt my leg, bad.'

Rory stood for a moment, wondering what to do.

'Where are your mates?'

'I don't know!' Craig snapped. 'And anyway, what's it to do with you?'

Rory shrugged and started to walk on.

'Wait.'

Rory stopped and looked back.

'Look, I'm sorry,' Craig said. 'It's just that … well, it's hurting real bad. Could you help me?'

Rory hesitated.

'What d'you want me to do?'

Craig pointed across the street to where a new-looking BMX bike rested against a wall. 'That's my brother's bike,' he said. 'There's no way I can ride it with my leg like this. Look at me – I can hardly walk.' He nodded towards a bus stop a little way down the street. 'But I can get a bus from over there.'

Rory glanced over at the BMX, wondering if it really did belong to Craig's brother.

Craig seemed to read his thoughts. 'It *is* my brother's

bike, honest. First time he's let me ride it and this happens. He'll murder me if I don't get it home safe.'

'So what can I do, then?' Rory asked.

'Will you ride it home for me?'

Rory looked at the bike again and then back at Craig. 'I don't know where you live.'

'It's not far. I'll give you the address. My brother's there now.'

'Why can't he come and get the bike then?'

'Look, I asked you to help!' Craig snapped. 'But if it's too much bother—'

'All right, I'll do it,' Rory said quickly. 'Tell me where you live.'

Craig gave Rory his address.

It was about three kilometres from where they were and Rory knew the way. He guessed that it wouldn't take him too long to deliver the bike and then walk home. 'See you, then,' he said, turning away to cross the street.

'Help me up, will you?' Craig asked.

Rory stopped and turned back. He leaned down, gripped one of Craig's arms and helped him slowly to his feet.

The other boy flinched and he tentatively put pressure on his injured leg. 'Hope I've not broken anything.'

'You want me to help you to the bus stop?' Rory asked.

'No,' Craig said. 'You get off with the bike.'

Rory nodded. 'See you, then.'

'Yeah, see you. And, thanks.'

'No bother.'

Rory walked across the street, and climbed onto the new BMX. He rode off the pavement onto the road and started to pedal away.

'Thanks again!' Craig shouted.

Rory looked back and raised an arm.

'That's right,' Craig whispered. 'Wave to the camera, Rory.'

Rory rang the doorbell. There was no sound from inside the house, so he guessed that the bell was broken. He knocked on the front door and waited.

He didn't know the area very well, but the house had been easy enough to find. The street was similar to many others in and around Edinburgh. Long rows of old, terraced houses sat behind low front walls and tiny gardens.

The garden to this house was nothing more than a small rectangle of paving slabs, most of them broken. Rory glanced down at the thin, straggling weeds poking through jagged cracks. It looked as though even the weeds struggled to survive in this part of the city.

The house itself seemed just as neglected as its garden. On the ground floor, faded blue paint was peeling away from the front door and a pane of glass in the single sash window had a crack running from one corner to another.

Upstairs, there were no curtains in the window. And higher still, the guttering had broken away from the downpipe and constantly dripping water had left an ugly, green stain on the dull brickwork.

Rory knocked again, louder than before, and this time footsteps thumped noisily down the staircase.

The door swung open and an angry-faced boy of about sixteen stood there scowling. 'What?'

Rory guessed the boy was Craig's brother. They both had pale skin, hard, narrow eyes and dark red hair.

'I brought your bike,' Rory said.

The boy didn't reply.

'Your bike,' Rory said again, nodding down at the BMX he was holding. 'Craig asked me to bring your bike home. He's hurt his leg.'

'Stupid little...' the other boy said. 'Give it here.'

He stepped outside, snatched the BMX and wheeled it into the house before turning back to Rory. Then he laughed and closed the door.

Taken aback, Rory stood there for a few moments, staring at the door. 'What was all that about?' he muttered, with a shake of his head.

Rory was angry, but he wasn't stupid. There was no point in knocking on the door and telling Craig's brother what he thought of him. He just had to let it go and get home. Hungry and tired, he walked quickly to the end of the street, turning left.

And then he came face to face with five boys on bikes.

It was Travis and his gang – including Craig. Their bikes were strung out in a line across the pavement and there was no way for Rory to get past without stepping into the road.

Travis was in the middle of the group. 'Hello, Rory,' he said. 'Thanks for being so helpful. We're very grateful.'

Craig sat on Travis's right, grinning his familiar evil grin. He was perched comfortably on his bike. There wasn't the slightest sign of an injured leg.

Rory realized that he'd been set up, but he couldn't work out why. 'What's going on?' he asked.

Travis pulled a mobile phone from his jacket pocket. He waved it at Rory. 'I just got a call from Craig's brother, telling me you delivered the bike safe and sound.'

'But it's not his bike, is it?' Rory said slowly. He nodded towards Craig. 'And there's nothing wrong with his leg.'

The five boys were all smiling. 'I made a miraculous recovery almost as soon as you rode away,' Craig said, smacking his leg with the palm of a hand. 'See, no worries. It's fine.'

'I'm fed up with playing stupid games,' Rory snapped, suddenly angry at being taken for a fool. 'I'm going home.'

'I think you'd better take a look at this little film I made,' Travis said.

Rory was just about to step into the road to avoid the boys, but Travis's words stopped him in his tracks.

'What film?'

'You didn't see me, but I was watching you all the time you were with Craig.'

'No, you weren't there. I'd have seen—'

Travis cut him short with a laugh. 'Oh, I was there, all right, behind the white van. Remember it? You were so busy looking at Craig that you walked straight past me.'

'Show him your movie, T,' Craig said. 'It's really good.'

'Yeah, come and take a look, Rory,' Travis added. 'I reckon it's one of the best I've ever made.'

Rory's heart was pounding as he walked over to Travis, who held up the phone so that the younger boy could see the screen.

'Watch closely,' Travis said, jabbing a finger at the screen.

Rory's mouth went dry as he watched the short film. He could be clearly seen walking across the road, getting onto the BMX bike and riding away. Travis had even managed to zoom in on him as he turned back to wave.

'Pretty good, eh?' Travis said. 'Nice close up of you at the end, too. Want to see it again?'

Rory shook his head. 'No, I don't.'

'Didn't think you would,' Travis said. His smile suddenly disappeared. 'We stole that bike two days ago, from exactly the same place you took it from. And now we've got a film of you stealing it. If you don't do what I say, this video's going to be all over the Internet. I think I'll label it, "Rory Temu, bike thief".'

Rory stared, terrified at what he was hearing. 'You're … you're kidding me, right?'

Travis shook his head slowly. 'No, I'm not kidding. You stole that bike, and I'm going to post the evidence online. I reckon the police'll come calling in a day or two. Your mum won't like that, will she?'

'I'll tell them,' Rory said, panic rising in his voice. 'I'll tell them it was you. I'll bring them here and show them the bike.'

'What bike?' Travis said innocently, turning to Craig. 'Go on, tell him.'

'It's gone,' Craig said. 'My brother's shifted it. You'll find nothing stolen at our house because we're a perfectly respectable family.'

The other boys were laughing.

'Whereas *you*, Rory,' Craig continued, 'are the son of a well-known loser who spends most of his time in prison for stealing.'

'What?' Rory gasped.

'Oh, it's easy to find out these things, just by asking around,' Travis said. 'Everyone knows about Eddie Temu. They reckon he's just about the worst burglar in the whole of Scotland. So who d'you the think the police will believe – nice, honest boys like me and Craig, or you?'

Rory couldn't reply. He was fighting back tears.

'They'll believe *us*,' Travis said. 'The police will see my film and they'll say, "Like father, like son." And then it'll be big, big trouble for Rory Temu.' Slipping his mobile into a pocket, he got off his bike and gave it to Craig to hold. Then he stepped over to Rory and put one arm around his shoulders. 'So,' he said quietly but firmly, 'you *will* be joining us, won't you?'

Rory said nothing. He just nodded meekly.

Nine

'You'd be amazed at how stupid most people are, Rory,' Travis said to the newest and youngest member of his gang. 'They think it won't happen to them, 'cos their bike is different to everyone else's and it won't get nicked. So they don't lock it. Makes our job even easier.'

The six-strong team were milling about the town on the lookout for targets and opportunities. Travis, Craig and Jackie were on bikes, while the others – Josh, Duncan and Rory – were on foot.

'We work together, that's the rule,' Travis said. 'Help each other out. That way, we don't get caught.'

Travis's words didn't make Rory feel any better. He was scared and bewildered, and felt sick to his stomach at what he was doing. But there was no alternative.

'Look, T,' Craig said suddenly. He nodded towards a mini-supermarket a little further down the street.

The six boys watched as a young man rested his bike against the wall of the building. He stuck a hand in his pocket, pulled out what looked like a wallet and then walked into the shop, leaving the bike unsecured.

'See what I mean, Rory?' Travis said. 'Stupid or what?'

Rory didn't get the chance to reply.

'Here we go, lads,' Travis went on quickly. 'Josh and Duncan, go after him. Rory, they'll hang about in the doorway for a bit and delay him if he comes back too soon. As soon as they're in position, you go and get the bike. You know where to take it. Me and Craig will follow you. Jackie's going to hang around here to see what happens. You got that?'

Rory nodded, his heart thudding in his chest.

'Let's go, then.'

Josh and Duncan walked casually across the street and stood in the shop doorway.

'Go, Rory! Now!' Travis said, pushing him into action.

Rory didn't have time to stop and think. He hurried across the road and, almost in a dream, pulled the bike away from the wall. He slid onto the saddle and hurtled away, weaving his way through the heavy traffic, petrified that at any moment he would hear a shout as the furious bike owner came tearing after him.

No one shouted and no one chased him. But, unknown to Rory, Travis was busy again with his phone's camera, filming the whole incident.

Fifteen minutes later, Rory was standing beside the bike in a quiet alleyway close to Craig's home. He was trembling. Thinking about what he had done made him feel ill.

He wasn't alone for long. Travis and Craig came riding up on their bikes, with the rest of the gang arriving on foot soon after.

The gang leader looked highly delighted with his latest recruit's lightning-fast getaway. 'You were brilliant, Rory,' Travis said. 'So fast. Even Craig couldn't have got away like that, especially in all that traffic.'

Craig glared as Travis spoke, but other members of the gang were keen to join in the praise.

'Didn't I tell you he'd be good?' Jackie said from under his baseball cap.

'You did, Jackie Boy.' Travis smiled. 'I can see that Rory is going to be our new star.'

'He was cool, all right,' Duncan said. 'We saw that from the shop.'

'Great,' Josh added. 'Amazing for a first-timer.'

Rory was burning with shame over what he had done, and every word of praise only made him feel worse.

Craig looked furious. 'We'd better shift the bike before anyone comes looking for it,' he said, quickly changing the subject.

Travis nodded. 'You and Jackie take it to the usual place, right?'

Craig grabbed the bike from Rory, and thrust it to Jackie who climbed on, ready to ride away.

'Can I go home now?' Rory muttered to Travis.

'Of course.' Travis smiled. 'You can go when you've had your first pay.'

'I don't want any money.'

'You've got to have money!' Travis snapped, suddenly angry. 'And stop whining. You're one of us now, so take this.' He pulled a crumpled ten-pound note from his pocket and held it out to Rory. 'Go on.'

The other boys' eyes widened.

'We don't usually get that much, T,' Josh muttered.

'Our new lad's done so well that I'm giving him a little bonus.' He turned back to Rory. 'It's yours.'

Slowly, Rory reached out and took the note. Then he thrust it into his pocket and went to leave.

'Wait a minute,' Travis barked. 'Be careful with the cash. Don't go splashing out on things or your mum will start asking questions.'

'And make sure your old man doesn't see it next time he gets out of prison.' Jackie laughed.

Travis was suddenly all smiles again. 'You'll soon get used to it,' he said to Rory. 'You'll like having the cash and you'll like doing what we do.'

'I'll never like it,' Rory said angrily.

Travis shrugged. 'Suit yourself. One of us will meet you outside school the next time you're needed.'

He grinned. 'Unless you want to hang out with us tomorrow?'

Rory shook his head and started to walk away.

The other boys smiled as they watched him go.

'Laters, Rory,' Travis called.

'Are you all right?'

Grace was standing by Rory's bedroom door. Her brother lay stretched out on his bed with his hands over his eyes.

'Rory?'

'I'm all right,' Rory said at last, without taking his hands from his eyes.

'You're not.'

Rory sprang from his bed and stormed over to his sister. 'I told you,' he snapped. 'I'm all right. Now leave me alone!'

Grace looked closely at him. 'There's something wrong, isn't there?'

'No, there isn't.'

'I've never seen you like this before. You look ... scared.'

'I am not scared!'

'Is it because Dad's coming home?'

'No! I told you, I'm not scared. I'm just... Oh, Grace, just leave me alone. Please.'

Grace studied him for a few more moments. Then she sighed. 'Okay, Rory,' she said sadly. 'I know there's something. But if you don't want my help...' She turned away and went quickly down the stairs.

Rory closed the bedroom door and flung himself face-down on the bed, feeling more miserable than he'd ever felt in his entire life.

He hung one arm over the edge of the mattress and patted his fingers under the bed until they came into contact with an old tin box that had once contained Christmas biscuits.

Now it was Rory's tin. If was like a little safe – the place where Rory kept his special things, including his lists.

His mum and his sister both knew that it was Rory's private tin, and they never touched it. Until now, it wouldn't really have mattered if they'd looked inside. Rory had never had anything to hide before.

But now he did.

Because inside the tin, among the lists and the photos and the medal his great-grandad had won many years ago and all the other things that were special to Rory, was the ten-pound note that Travis had given him.

And as Rory touched the tin and thought of the money, tears filled his eyes and slowly trickled onto his pillow.

Ten

Phil Jacks and Richard Vaughton stood close to the start gate as the riders prepared for the race.

'Is the lad okay?' Phil asked. 'He looks very tired. And he's so quiet – nothing like the first time he was here.'

Mr Vaughton nodded. 'Maybe it's nerves, but he's been tense for days. Really edgy.'

'We don't want to get Rory into the sport if it affects him like this,' Phil said. 'He's meant to enjoy it.'

'I'm not absolutely sure it's racing that's worrying him,' Mr Vaughton said slowly.

'What, then?'

Mr Vaughton hesitated for a moment. 'Rory's mum came to see me at school the other day,' he said. 'His dad is being released from prison very soon and Mrs Temu thinks it's playing on Rory's mind. He doesn't get on with his dad.'

Phil sighed. 'Thanks for telling me. We'll give the lad any support we can if he needs it. I'm sure you'll do the same at school.'

'Sure,' Mr Vaughton said. 'But so far Rory's said nothing. He probably doesn't want to talk about it.'

Up at the gate, the riders were ready for the start. Rory was trying hard to concentrate, but he felt terrible. This was meant to be his big day. It was his first serious race against other novice riders. But the sport that had been so thrilling a few days earlier hardly mattered to him at all now, not when he had so many other things on his mind.

All Rory could think about was the web of crime he'd been drawn into and couldn't escape. He hated the feeling of being trapped. But most of all, he hated knowing that what he was doing was plain wrong.

Rory sat on his bike, staring down at the ground. He was kitted out with a helmet and gloves, as well as elbow pads and knee pads under his clothes. He looked like a racer, even though he didn't feel like one.

'Okay, riders, let's set 'em up!'

The command to get into position sent ripples of excitement along the trackside. Members of the club and BMX race fans had been tipped to watch out for the youngster who had the makings of a star.

But Rory was struggling even to remember what to do. He tried to think back to the videos he had seen of BMX stars Shanaze Reade and Liam Phillips, telling himself to be like them – totally focused, determined and mind set in the racing zone.

He had to ride well for Mr Vaughton, Phil and everyone else at the club who'd been so kind. His mum and sister had wanted to come and watch him race, but Rory had put them off, saying that they would make him nervous.

Riders ready!

Eight riders edged their bikes up to the gate, settled in their lanes and stared down the track towards the first berm.

Watch the gate!

This was the moment Rory had so looked forward to – his real first race. The beeps began. But Rory's mind was in turmoil and his vision was as blurred as his thoughts. Was that the first beep or the second? And that one, was it—?

Suddenly the gate crashed down and as the other riders leapt away, Rory was left sitting absolutely motionless. He'd missed the start. Panicking, he pushed away, pedalling frantically and trying to make up the time he'd thrown away.

He was easily the last of the riders at the berm, where he leaned too hard and wobbled, almost tumbling to the ground. And he was still in last place as the other riders sailed over the bumps.

Rory was desperate to improve his position or at

the very least not to finish last. He drove hard at the pedals and, with a sudden burst of speed, passed one rider to go into seventh place.

At the trackside, Mr Vaughton and Phil exchanged a look.

'A bit better,' Phil said. 'But he's not right.'

Rory leapt over a bump, gaining quickly on another rider. They reached the second berm together and Rory took the outside line, attempting to pass his rival on the bend. But as he leaned over, Rory felt his back wheel slide away, totally out of control, and the next thing he knew, he was laying on the track in the dirt.

He scrambled quickly to his feet and clambered back onto his bike. The other riders were so far away now that there was no chance of getting back into the race. But Rory began pedalling, knowing that he had to make it to the finish line, even in last position.

The other riders had ended their race before Rory even turned into the final straight. The finish line suddenly looked miles away. His legs felt leaden and every turn of the pedals became hard work.

At last, though, Rory crossed the line with sympathetic applause from a few spectators pounding in his ears. He rode on until he found a quiet spot and came to a halt, staring down at the ground and feeling totally alone.

There was a gentle pat on his shoulders and Rory

looked up and saw a boy of his own age, called Donny, that he had become friendly with.

Donny was a much more experienced BMX racer and had loaned Rory the elbow pads and knee pads that he was wearing. He smiled sympathetically. 'Don't worry about it,' he said with a shrug. 'My first race was just as bad. You'll be fine next time.'

Rory shook his head. 'No,' he said firmly. 'I was useless ... terrible. I'm never doing that again.'

Eleven

'Hey, son,' Eddie Temu said, 'I've missed you. Come over here and give your dad a hug.' He spread his arms wide and waited.

Rory didn't move. He'd listened to Eddie's voice booming through the tiny house for more than half an hour before he'd gone downstairs. And even then, he'd wanted to stay in his bedroom. But he didn't want to upset his mum and sister.

No way was he hugging him though.

Eddie was sitting at the kitchen table, wearing a broad smile and looking like a king in his court.

'Not too grown up to give your old dad a hug, are you?' Eddie asked, flashing the irritating grin that was imprinted on Rory's memory.

'I'm not a kid any more,' Rory said quietly.

Eddie's smile faded. 'I can see that. You've grown. Two years is a long time.'

Two years.

It *was* a long time. It meant that Rory hadn't seen his

dad since he was ten. But as far as he was concerned, two years wasn't long enough. He would be happy if he never saw Eddie again.

Rory still didn't move. But he saw the anxiety on his mum's face, and on Grace's face, too.

'Go on, Rory,' Mary urged. 'Give your dad a hug.'

Eddie nodded, smiling sadly this time. His face was suddenly childlike, as if he were a little boy lost.

Rory felt jolt of anger. There was a sour taste in his mouth and he wanted to spit it out. He remembered this look, too, and all the play-acting that went with it – Eddie behaving as though everyone should feel sorry for him, because none of his crimes were really his fault. But as he sat at the kitchen table, his arms outstretched, Eddie reminded Rory of a big spider, trying to lure a fly into its web and trap it there.

Rory glanced towards his sister, who nodded very slightly and that was when he knew that he had to do as his mum had asked. It was the only way to keep the peace in this house.

He edged slowly forward, stepping into Eddie's embrace and allowing the big man to wrap him in his enormous arms.

'That's better,' Eddie breathed into his son's ear as he gripped him tightly. Too tightly. Rory *was* trapped; the breath was being squeezed from his lungs. And he knew his dad was doing it deliberately, reminding his son who was the boss.

Rory didn't struggle. He just waited, telling himself that even though Eddie seemed to have convinced his mum yet again, he wouldn't fool Rory and he wouldn't fool Grace.

Finally, the pressure eased as Eddie relaxed his grip. Rory stepped back quickly, just out of reach.

Eddie was grinning as he turned to Mary. 'We're one big happy family again, just like I dreamed we'd be.'

Mary smiled and nodded, as Rory watched his dad turn his attention to Grace. 'And your mum's been telling me what a genius you are. You must get it from me.' He laughed out loud. 'How about you make your old dad his first cup of tea of freedom? Then you can tell him all about it.'

Grace didn't reply. She just picked up the kettle and went to the sink to fill it.

Rory couldn't bear to listen to any more. 'Have to do my homework,' he muttered, walking quickly from the room before any one could stop him.

As Rory stomped up the stairs, he heard his dad say loudly, 'Homework? When did Rory start doing homework?'

Later that day, Rory was sitting with his sister in her bedroom. They were saying very little, their dad's voice still echoing in their heads.

Eddie was downstairs, talking to Mary. Every so often they would hear another peal of laughter.

'Boasting about his big plans, no doubt,' Grace said at last. 'He asked me one thing about school and when I started to answer he butted in and totally ignored what I was saying. Again. It's driving me crazy and he's only just got back.'

Rory didn't reply. He was deep in his own thoughts.

'And what about the way he talks about himself as if he's someone else?' Grace said. 'It's weird. I can't stand the way he calls himself, "your old dad," like he's not there.' Grace looked at her brother, as if waiting for a reply.

Eventually Rory realized that he was meant to answer. 'I hate him, Grace,' he said darkly.

'I know you do,' said Grace. 'You're not very good at hiding it. But if we're lucky, maybe he won't be here for long.'

Rory sighed. 'I'm not lucky. I've never been lucky.'

'What?'

'Nothing,' Rory said, shaking his head.

'Come on, what do you mean?'

'I don't mean anything,' Rory said. 'I was just

saying... I just meant... I don't...' The words died in his mouth as he realized that he'd said too much already. Anything more he said could only make the situation worse.

'Rory, what is going on?' Grace said. 'You look worried all the time, and it's not just Dad, is it?'

'Don't start, Grace,' Rory snapped, jumping to his feet. 'It's bad enough having him here. I don't need you getting at me as well.'

'I want to help you.'

'I don't need help!' Without another word, Rory stormed out.

'Rory?' Grace whispered.

Twelve

Rory was good at stealing, so good that Travis was ordering him to do it more and more often. In a few, short weeks, Rory had become his number-one operator.

But Rory was scared. He was scared of Travis and of Craig, too. Every time the gang leader heaped more words of praise on his newest recruit, Rory saw the hatred that burned in the former favourite's eyes.

Late one Thursday afternoon, Rory was riding home. He'd stolen another bike that day and delivered it to the rest of the gang. There was more money in his pocket, as well as the pay-as-you-go mobile Travis had given him a few days earlier.

'It's so we can keep in touch,' Travis had told him. 'My number's on there. Call or text when you want, and I'll do the same.'

Rory had never owned a mobile phone, but he'd always wanted one. Yet now that he had a mobile, he didn't want it. It was another tie to the gang – another reminder of the life he'd been dragged into.

He rode through the gates of the park feeling weary. Even the joy of simply riding his BMX had drained away. He hated what he was doing and what he'd become: a thief, just like his dad. But he didn't have a choice, did he? And there was no one he could turn to for help.

As he pedalled along the tarmac path, Rory was thinking that his new life might mean that he had more money than ever before, but what he earned was of no use to him. He was too ashamed to spend any of the cash or give it to his mum or his sister. Every penny he'd received was hidden away in the tin beneath his bed. And the money in his pocket would join it when he got home.

He felt almost tearful as he thought of his tin and the special memories associated with everything in it. They were all spoiled now, tainted by Travis's money.

'Just like I am,' Rory whispered.

He reached the end of the path, got off his bike and wheeled it around the bollard and through the exit. He couldn't be bothered to ride through at high speed like he usually did; he didn't have the energy.

When he got home, he locked his bike in the shed and went to the back door as usual. It was locked, but Rory wasn't surprised about that. His mum was at work and recently Grace had been staying late at school or going to a friend's place to do her homework. It was stressful being at home with their dad around.

Eddie was obviously out. That was no surprise either. None of them ever knew when he would be at home.

Rory used his key to get in, glad that he was alone in the house and that there would be plenty of time to hide away the money before anyone came home. He slipped off his trainers and padded through the kitchen to the hallway.

As he climbed the stairs, a dream from the previous night flashed into his mind. He'd had it several times now, and it always started well. He was a top BMX racer – a star – riding with some of the great names in the sport.

Rory shuddered as he remembered the details. He'd been racing for Team GB, riding over the London 2012 course and going for Olympic glory. Every metre of the course, every turn of the wheel and every smiling face in the crowd had been in dazzling colour.

Rory was at the front, with the crowd shouting his name as he approached the final corner. He slid into the bend and effortlessly straightened up, ready to fly down the final straight and claim Olympic gold.

And then, just as always, the dream became a nightmare. Rory was no longer leading the race over the Olympic course, he was out on the streets and the bike he was riding was stolen. And he was being chased, hunted down. The shouts and cheers of the crowd had turned to angry cries.

'Thief!'

'Stop!'

'Get him!'

The smiling, happy faces were now ugly and angry. It was horrible and all so vividly real.

Rory gasped in panic and for one terrifying instant, he didn't know where he was. Then he looked around and found himself at the top of the stairs, clinging to the banister rail. He was gripping it so tightly that he could see the whites of his knuckles. This was stupid. He couldn't go on like this.

He stood for a moment, breathing deeply, forcing the nightmare from his mind. He took the few steps towards his bedroom, grasped the handle and pushed open the door. Then he stopped and stared.

His dad was sitting on his bed.

'Hello, Rory,' he said.

Thirteen

Eddie sat back on the bed, Rory's secret tin wide open
on his lap. And all the money that had been hidden at
the bottom of the tin was gripped in Eddie's hands. He
smiled. 'Well, boy,' he said quietly. 'That's quite a lot
of money you've got here. You going to tell your old
dad how you got it?'

Rory swallowed. He didn't know what to say.

'I'm waiting,' Eddie said. 'Where did you get it?'

Desperately, Rory tried to think of a way of
explaining where the cash had come from.

'I... I... I earned it.'

Eddie raised his eyebrows. 'Oh, really? And how
exactly did you earn it?'

'I've been working.'

'Doing what?'

'A ... a paper round.'

Eddie smiled. 'Maybe you can get me a paper
round.' He opened his hands, revealing the crumpled
notes. 'I've never heard of a paper round that pays this

well.' Then he was suddenly serious. 'Come on, Rory,' he snapped. 'Where d'you get it?'

Before Rory could blurt out another lie, his mobile began to ring.

'Oh.' Eddie laughed. 'So you've got a phone, too. You really have come into money.'

Rory didn't move as the ringing continued.

'You going to answer that? Could be important.'

Rory shook his head. The phone rang on and on. Finally, it stopped.

'Give me that phone,' Eddie said, breaking the sudden silence.

Rory shook his head again.

'Give it to me, Rory.' The words were menacing.

Slowly and reluctantly Rory reached into his pocket, took out the phone and handed it over.

Eddie studied the screen for a few moments. 'Travis called,' he said. 'Maybe I should call Travis back and ask him if he knows how you got all this money. What d'you think?'

'No, don't,' Rory said quickly. 'Please don't. I'll tell you.'

'Yeah, thought you might,' Eddie said. He waited.

Rory's face was burning with shame. 'I ... I've been stealing things.'

'Well, well, well,' Eddie said quietly. 'Go on, son.'

Feeling as though he was about to fall down, Rory

leaned back against the wall. Slowly, he explained how he'd been tricked into joining the gang and how they stole bikes and sold them on for cash.

For once, Eddie didn't interrupt. He just listened, nodding occasionally, but saying nothing. When Rory had finished his story, Eddie nodded a few times more, appearing to be weighing up what he'd been told.

'Clever boy, this Travis,' he said at last. 'Sounds like he's got a good business going.'

'Are you going to tell Mum?' Rory asked, without looking at his dad.

Eddie shrugged. 'Not necessarily. Not unless I have to. It's probably best your mum and sister don't ever learn about this. We both know how hurt they'd be. Don't we?'

Rory nodded. He watched as his dad slipped the cash into his pocket.

'No,' Eddie said. 'I think it's best if you go on doing exactly what you've been doing. I'll say nothing and we can divide the money you make – some for you, some for me.'

'I don't want it,' Rory said.

Eddie shrugged. 'You'll do what I say, Rory. For now, you just keep working with Travis, and I'll keep my mouth—'

A sudden noise from downstairs stopped Eddie from continuing. Then footsteps sounded on the stairs.

'Rory?' Grace called. 'Are you up there?'

Eddie nodded for him to answer.

'I'm in my room,' Rory said.

They heard footsteps on the stairs and then Grace appeared in the doorway.

'Dad!' she gasped, looking completely shocked to see Eddie sitting on the bed. 'What are you doing in here?'

Eddie smiled. 'I'm spending some quality time with my son.' He winked. 'Eh, Rory?'

Rory nodded, forcing a thin smile to his lips.

'That's his special tin you've got,' Grace said. 'No one ever looks inside.'

'Then I'm privileged,' Eddie replied. 'It was Rory's idea.'

Grace looked at her brother. 'Is that true?' she asked. 'Did you want Dad to do that?'

Rory shrugged. 'Yeah. There's nothing to hide in there. You can look in it if you want.'

Grace stared at her dad, who was smiling.

'No, thanks,' Grace said. 'I don't want to see in your tin.'

Fourteen

'Okay, Rory,' Travis said. 'Dunc and Josh reckon this guy turns up here most nights around six, and he always stays for at least an hour. So you've got plenty of time. But get the bike and get away quick. We don't want any nosy neighbours butting in. You got that?'

'Got it,' Rory answered, looking across the road to the row of smart houses nestling behind low iron railings.

'He takes his bike through the gate and just leaves it in the little front garden, against the railings. No lock, no chain, nothing. He must think this is an honest neighbourhood.' Travis laughed.

Rory stayed silent.

'It's just you and Craig today,' Travis went on. 'The others are in town, on another little job. But don't worry, Rory. Craig'll see you're all right. Eh, Craig?'

Craig was sitting on his BMX. He stared across the street, his eyes as cold as ever. 'Yeah, I'll take care of him.'

Travis was already riding away. 'I'll see you both later, in the park. With the bike.'

Rory watched him go. 'Never does any stealing himself, does he?' he muttered. 'Always leaves it to us.'

Craig shrugged. 'He's the boss. And I wouldn't let him hear you say that if I were you.'

The quiet road was tree-lined and wide, very different to the streets where Rory and Craig lived.

They waited in silence, and Rory began hoping that maybe the cyclist wouldn't turn up and he wouldn't have to steal the bike after all. But his hopes were dashed when Craig nudged him with one elbow and gestured towards the end of the road.

A cyclist was approaching, riding slowly on an expensive-looking bike. He reached the gate and just as Travis had predicted pushed his bike through and leaned it against the railings, without securing it in any way.

'Mug,' Craig breathed. 'We'll wait till he's inside, then go and get it. I'll be behind you, following.'

Rory knew the routine well by now.

The two boys watched as the man rang the doorbell and was let into the house. And then Craig was prodding Rory into action. 'Let's go.'

Rory wanted to get it over with, so he didn't hesitate. He walked quickly across the road, went through the open gate, grabbed the bike by the handlebars and wheeled it out into the street. The frame was quite large, but he knew that he could handle it.

There was no one around. This was going to be so easy. Rory pushed off, wobbling slightly. The bike was bigger than he'd thought, but both of his feet were on the pedals and he was off, searching for a higher gear so that he could move more quickly.

'Hey, you! Stop!'

Rory heard the shout and glanced back. It wasn't the bike's owner. A man had come running out of the house next door.

'Stop!'

Rory felt a surge of panic, but he found the right gear and gained speed, certain that if he kept pedalling he would soon leave the man trailing far behind.

He looked back again and saw Craig riding fast and hard, quickly passing the pursuer. Rory breathed a little easier; they were both going to escape.

'Stop! Thief! Stop!'

Rory changed gear for a second time. He was going even quicker now. Out of the corner of his eye, he saw Craig alongside.

Suddenly, he felt a vicious punch on one arm that sent him tumbling sideways. He lost control and crashed down onto the road, rolling over as the bike bounced and then skidded away.

Rory's head was spinning as he tried to stagger to

his feet, knowing that he had to run.

But it was too late.

'Got you!'

Two hands grasped Rory's arms, holding him tightly, and then pinning him to the ground, making absolutely certain that there would be no escape.

But Rory didn't even struggle. He knew it was pointless. Further down the road, he glimpsed Craig disappearing around a corner as other neighbours emerged from their houses, drawn by the shouting.

'I saw him do it,' the man shouted as the bike's owner came running up. 'I saw him steal your bike and I wasn't going to let him get away. You'd better call the police.'

Fifteen

It had been the worst few days of Rory's life. Questions and tears at the police station led to even more questions and upset at school and at home.

Rory's nightmares had become reality.

He told the police everything, relieved that the truth could be brought out into the open at last. He told how he had been tricked into stealing for the gang and how he'd been terrified that if he didn't do as Travis ordered, the films of him taking bikes would be posted on the Internet. He told the names of the other gang members and Craig's address. Finally, he told how the gang operated.

But Rory kept one secret from everyone.

The warning glances from his dad were followed by threatening, whispered words, telling him to keep his mouth shut. So Rory never mentioned that Eddie had taken the money from his tin and ordered him to carry on stealing. He knew that if his mum found out, she would be completely heartbroken. So Rory left out that part of the story, hoping that that Eddie would leave him alone now the supply of cash had dried up.

A few days later, Rory and his mum were at school, sitting in Mr Vaughton's office with the teacher and a police liaison officer called WPC Amber McInnes.

'So, Rory,' the police officer said, 'you're certain there's nothing else you've got to tell us?'

Eddie's smiling face flashed briefly into Rory's mind, but he shook his head. 'Nothing.'

'Okay, good,' WPC McInnes said. 'You know that you've been lucky, don't you?'

Rory didn't feel very lucky, but he nodded anyway.

'When Mr Jameson – whose bike you took – heard the full facts, he decided that he didn't want to press charges. And as this is your first time in trouble, you get an official warning from us. But I don't want you to think that you've just got away with it. We'll be watching you in future. You know that, too, don't you?'

Rory was staring at the desktop in front of him. 'I do,' he said softly.

'Right,' WPC McInnes said more kindly, 'let's

talk about the future. From what I've seen and been told, there are a lot of people who want to help you, including your teacher here.'

She turned to Mr Vaughton, who had been waiting for his chance to speak.

'We'd all like you to come back to the cycling club, Rory,' the teacher said. 'Now we know what's been going on, it's easy to see why you made such a mess of that first race, and why you didn't want to think about racing afterwards. Your mind must have been all over the place.'

Rory nodded. 'It was, sir.'

'We think you've got really great potential as a BMX racer, Rory.' He sat forward on his chair, as if anxious for Rory's answer. 'So, what do you reckon?'

For the first time in what seemed like an age, Rory felt a smile of real happiness spread across his face. 'I'd love that, sir,' he said. 'I'd really love it.'

Mary reached across, took one of her son's hands in hers and looked at the police officer. 'What about those boys?' she said anxiously. 'They won't don't do anything to hurt Rory, will they?

WPC McInnes shook her head. 'I don't think so. We haven't been able to prove anything against Travis and his gang. And we've found none of the stolen items. Not yet. But they'll make a mistake. We'll catch them eventually.'

Sixteen

Rory was battling up the second long straight, a broad smile fixed on his face.

He went soaring over a bump – one of the wave-like bumps in the track – and headed for the final berm, just in the lead.

On the trackside, Phil Jacks turned to Richard Vaughton and raised his eyebrows. 'This is terrific,' he said. 'He's beating some really experienced racers here. Young Donny out there's our top man in this age group.'

Mr Vaughton watched eagerly, delighted that Rory was back where he belonged and proving just how good he could be. 'I thought all along that Rory could be special,' he said.

'Let's see how he manages the last turn and the finish,' Phil said, not taking his eyes from the track. 'This is where nerves often get to the newcomers.'

If Rory was feeling nervous, it didn't show. He neared the berm and prepared to lean into it, with the other riders scrambling to keep up and jostling for position.

But racing at this level was still quite new to Rory and he went into the turn a little further across the track than was perfect for cornering.

It gave the rider in second place the opportunity to snatch the inside line and close the gap between them to no distance at all. They were neck and neck.

'See, too wide on the berm,' Phil said. 'Looks like Donny's going to get him now.'

But Rory was determined to battle all the way to the finish. He powered on, driving the pedals hard, his legs pumping like pistons.

'Go, Rory, go!' Mr Vaughton shouted, unable to stop himself from yelling.

Phil laughed. 'He's going to get it. He's going to win.'

Rory went streaking ahead. Speeding up the final straight, he crossed the line a bike's length ahead of Donny, who followed in second place.

'Fantastic!' Phil said. 'He's got an amazing burst of speed for someone his age and size. And that's made my mind up. He's going to the area championships.'

As Rory and Donny rode off the course together, Phil and Mr Vaughton watched them from the trackside. Donny raised one arm and the boys exchanged a high five. Even from a distance their laughter and excited chatter could clearly be heard.

'It's good to see that Rory's made a friend here, too,' Mr Vaughton said.

Donny's a fine lad,' Phil replied. 'He'll be a great mate to young Rory – just the sort of friend he needs.' He grinned. 'Won't stop Donny trying to beat him next time though.'

Rory was stretched out on his bed. He had just finished writing out a new 'People I like … and people I DON'T' list and was studying it closely. There had been a lot of changes, but there was no surprise there. Rory's life had changed a lot in the past few weeks.

His eyes flicked down the list from top to bottom.

	1. Mum
	2. Grace
	3 & 4. Nan and Grandad
	5. Mr Vaughton
	6. Donny
○	7. Adam
	8. CRAIG
	9. TRAVIS
	10. EDDIE

At the top, as always, were his mum and Grace. Rory had left out the 'most of the time' next to Grace's name. Throughout all the upset of the past few weeks she had not uttered a single word against her brother. Grace, Rory had decided, was the best sister around. And after all his help and support, Mr Vaughton had moved up the rankings, too.

Then there was a new arrival – Donny. The two boys were from very different backgrounds and different parts of the city, but had become firm friends. When they weren't racing or practising, they were usually talking about their bikes. And they always had a laugh, which was just what Rory needed right now. His new friend had helped him put his awful experiences to the back of his mind.

Things were much better now. Rory had seen nothing of Travis and his gang, and wondered if they were deliberately lying low or had moved their operations to another part of the city. He didn't really care where they were, as long as they didn't bother him.

Best of all, there was the news that Phil Jacks was entering Rory in his first championship event. It was a step in the right direction. Rory knew that it was only a small step, but everyone – Sir Chris Hoy, Shanaze Reade and Liam Phillips – had all taken the first-championship step once, just as Rory was about to do.

Rory's happiness dimmed slightly and he frowned as he read the bottom three names on his list – the dislikes. The new names at numbers eight and nine didn't matter as long as they left him alone, but the name at the very bottom remained the same. Eddie was a constant reminder of the recent bad times.

He sat up, carefully folded the list and placed it into his biscuit tin, which he pushed under the bed, wondering if his dad had delved into it recently. Probably not, he thought. Now that there was no cash, Eddie wouldn't be interested.

Rory went downstairs to get himself a drink. As he went into the kitchen he saw that the back door was open. Quickly slipping on his trainers, he went outside and heard noises coming from inside the shed.

He went over and peered inside. Eddie, with his back to the door, was bent double, rooting around among the old tins of paint, the stepladder, pieces of wood and other things that had been stored and forgotten.

'Dad?'

Surprised, Eddie stood up quickly, cracking his head on the underside of a shelf. 'Ow!' he yelled.

Rory wanted to laugh, but he bit his lip instead. 'You all right?'

'No, I'm not!' Eddie barked, rubbing the top of his head and grimacing in pain. 'What are you doing, sneaking up on me like that?'

'I didn't sneak,' Rory said. 'I walked.'

'Well, I didn't hear you. You should walk louder.'

'What are you doing in there?'

'Nothing,' Eddie growled. 'Just looking, that's all.'

Rory shook his head as he realized what his dad was up to. He was searching for things he could sell. He'd done it before. Like a thieving magpie, he took anything he thought would raise a few pounds.

'There's nothing in there worth any money, Dad,' Rory said. 'Apart from my bike.'

Eddie glared at his son. And then the glare turned into a sneering grin. 'Don't worry, I won't steal your bike. I don't steal bikes, not like some people we know.'

Rory felt himself blush at his dad's jibe. But he told himself not to get into an argument over it.

Eddie glanced at Rory's BMX. 'I don't know why you're wasting your time with all that racing stuff,' he snapped. 'Biking won't get you anywhere. You should be out there in the real world, doing stuff. It's a tough life. You've got to grab what you can.'

Rory had had enough of his dad's boasts and insults and threats. 'What, and be like you, Dad?' he said. 'No, thanks.'

Eddie's eyes blazed and he took a step towards his son. 'You little—'

'I've kept quiet for you,' Rory said quickly, 'for

mum's sake. But if you threaten me once more, I'll tell them that you took my money. And that you made me carry on stealing.'

'You wouldn't...'

'I would. You watch me.'

Father and son stared at each other for a few moments, but this time Rory wasn't scared and he wasn't backing down.

Finally Eddie shrugged his shoulders. 'Do what you like,' he said. 'I've got plans. Big plans. You'll see.'

But Rory didn't want to listen to any more. He went back to the house, turning to look over his shoulder as he reached the step. 'Make sure you lock the shed door when you've finished in there,' he called.

Seventeen

Rain pounded against the window and the wind howled and moaned. Rory pulled the duvet over his head, trying block out the early morning light squeezing through the gap in the curtains.

But he couldn't go back to sleep. And as he lay there, he realized that it wasn't just the noise of the wind and rain that had woken him. There was another sound – a banging that came every so often.

Rory closed his eyes, then immediately opened them as the banging noise came again, louder this time. It sounded just like an open window banging against its frame in the wind. But it couldn't be a window – no one would have left a window open in this weather. A door, then? But the front and back doors were always locked last thing at night. No, it must be something else.

Rory sat up as the banging sounded yet again. His bedroom window overlooked the back yard. Quickly, he pulled open the curtains and peered outside.

The weather was so bad that rainwater was pouring from the shed roof. But that wasn't all. The door was open, swinging backwards and forwards in the wind. And as Rory watched, it slammed once again against the doorframe.

'I told him to lock that door,' Rory muttered.

It was warm in the bedroom and Rory really didn't want to go outside into the wind and rain. He thought about diving under the duvet, pulling it over his head and trying to ignore the noise. But he knew it would be impossible.

So he got up, crept out of his room and padded quietly down the stairs to the kitchen, where he pulled on his jacket and trainers. Then he unlocked the door to go outside.

The rain was teeming down. Large puddles had formed on the paving slabs and Rory trod cautiously to the shed. He grabbed the swinging wooden door and went to close it.

Then he stopped. As he stared into the gloom of the shed, he knew instantly.

His BMX was gone.

'I didn't take your bike! What would I want with a kid's bike?'

Rory glared at his dad, who sat back on a kitchen chair and sipped from a mug of tea.

The whole family was up and out of bed now, roused by the noise Rory had made racing back into the house and shouting out at the top of his voice that his bike had been stolen.

'I saw you in the shed,' Rory hissed, 'searching for things to sell. You said that you wouldn't take my bike.'

'And I didn't,' Eddie growled. 'As far as I know, there's only one bike thief in this family.'

'Eddie!' Mary said sharply. 'There's no need to say that. We all know why Rory did what he did. And it's all over now.'

Eddie shrugged his shoulders and said nothing.

'What did you do with my bike?' Rory almost shouted. 'Tell me!'

Eddie looked over at his wife and raised both his hands in a gesture of innocence. 'What do I do?' He turned back to Rory. 'I didn't touch your stupid bike! Didn't go near it. I've told you all that I've changed. I don't steal any more.'

Rory was fuming. He'd had enough. He wasn't afraid of his dad any more, and he wasn't afraid to reveal the secret they shared.

94

But before Rory could speak, Eddie put down his mug and raised both hands again. This time, though, it looked as if he was about to confess.

The rest of the family waited for him to speak.

Eddie spoke slowly. 'I *may* – and I'm not saying that I definitely did – have forgotten to lock the shed door yesterday.'

'But I especially told you to lock it!' Rory gasped. 'I told you to make sure!'

'And maybe I did,' Eddie said, with another shrug. 'But maybe I didn't. I can't be certain. I've got a lot on my mind right now. So maybe if the shed door was *accidentally* left unlocked, someone else came along and stole the bike.' He shook his head sadly. 'There's a lot of dishonest people around.'

Rory wasn't convinced. 'Who?' he said, angrily. 'Who else would have taken it?'

'Maybe it was those old friends of yours,' Eddie replied, grinning.

Eddie's words silenced the room for a few moments. Then Grace took a step forward.

'Dad,' she said softly, 'is this the truth? Are you honestly telling us that you didn't take Rory's bike?'

Eddie sighed and his face took on a hurt look. 'I'm sad that you even feel you have to ask me, Gracie. But it's the truth. I'm telling you all, here and now, that I didn't take the bike.'

His eyes shifted to Rory. 'And I told you before, son. It's a tough world out there. Where's your bike racing got you now, eh?'

Eighteen

Rory was pretty certain that he would never see his bike again. He was less certain whether his dad was telling the truth or not. Perhaps he had just left the shed door open. But it didn't really matter either way. The bike was gone and there was no money for a replacement.

And as BMX bikes weren't cheap, it didn't look as though Rory would be racing or even riding again for a long time. His dreams had been shattered once more.

Three days later, there was still no sign of the missing bike. At break time, Rory wandered across the school yard with Adam, telling him that there was no news.

'So are you going to get another bike?' Adam asked.

Rory sighed. 'Can't afford it.'

'Can I have a word, Rory?'

Rory turned around to see Mr Vaughton approaching.

'I'm sorry, sir.'

'What?' said the teacher. 'What about?'

'My homework. I meant to do it last night, but—'

'For once, Rory,' Mr Vaughton said, interrupting, 'I'm not after your homework.'

'Oh.'

'Although I should be.' He smiled. 'No, this time I wanted to know if you'll be at the BMX track this evening?'

Rory shrugged. 'I don't know, really. Donny will be there, but with no bike to ride, I'd feel a bit stupid just hanging around.'

'So, you'd rather stay at home and do your English homework, would you?

Rory smiled. 'I didn't say that.'

'Get yourself down there, then,' Mr Vaughton said. 'You know that it's Donny's birthday on Sunday, don't you?'

'He didn't tell me.'

'No?' the teacher said. 'Well, Phil Jacks and some of the riders have bought him a birthday cake. They're giving it to him tonight, so you'd better come along and get yourself a slice.'

Rory wasn't really in the mood for celebrations, but he didn't want to let Donny down. 'Okay, I'll be there.'

Mr Vaughton nodded and went to go, but then

he stopped and turned back. 'Oh, and thanks for reminding me. Homework by next lesson.' He smiled. 'Or else!'

There was very little left of the BMX-shaped birthday cake. Everyone had enjoyed a slice and a few club members had managed at least two.

Only the back wheel, decorated in bright blue icing, remained.

'Want some more?' Donny asked Rory.

'I'm stuffed,' Rory answered, shaking his head.

'Not even a nice blue tyre? Or a spoke?'

'Nothing.' Rory laughed. 'You'll have to take the rest home.'

Donny grinned. 'I'm getting a cake on my birthday, too. D'you want to come over to mine on Sunday for another slice? You could see my presents and say hello to my parents. They're not bad, really, as parents go.'

'That'd be cool.' Rory smiled. 'Do you know what you're getting for your birthday?'

Donny suddenly looked a little embarrassed and glanced over to the far side of the track where Phil Jacks and Richard Vaughton were tidying up.

'I'm glad you asked me that,' Donny said to Rory. 'You see, I was going to wait until Christmas, or maybe next year, but I've asked my parents if I can have a new BMX now, and they've said I can.'

'A new one,' Rory said, his eyes widening. 'But the one you've already got is brilliant.'

'Yeah, it's not bad,' Donny agreed. 'That's why I thought if I got a new one…' He hesitated.

'What?' Rory asked. 'You'll have one for racing and one for riding? Great idea. That means you can keep one set up just for racing.'

Donny raised his eyes. 'No, you great wuss! I meant that *you* can have the old one.'

'Me?' Rory gasped.

'My parents think it's a great idea. So do Phil and Richard. And so do I.'

'But… But…'

'You're my mate,' Donny said. 'I want you to have it. And anyway, how can I beat you in the regionals if you haven't got a bike to ride?'

Rory stood staring, his mouth gaping wide.

'You'd better close your mouth.' Donny grinned. 'Or do you want me to shove another slice of cake in there after all?'

Nineteen

'It's well posh around here, eh?' Travis said, looking up and down the wide street.

Large detached houses sat behind neatly trimmed hedges. New, expensive-looking cars were parked in most of the driveways.

'Yeah, it is,' Craig replied.

'Too posh for the likes of us, eh, T?' Jackie laughed, tipping his baseball cap further back on his head.

'You speak for yourself, Jackie Boy,' Travis snapped. 'And who said you could call me T?'

'But you… I thought…'

'It's Travis, till I say different.'

'Right. Sorry, Travis. I just thought—'

'Shut up, Jackie Boy.'

Jackie fell silent.

Travis was in a bad mood. Again. Ever since Rory had escaped from his clutches and spoiled the smooth running of his thieving operation, Travis was almost always in a bad mood.

'Rory's done well in finding himself a friend who lives here,' Travis said to no one in particular. 'But we'll ruin that for him. I'll make him sorry for grassing us up to the police.'

'He's a coward as well as a grass, T,' Craig said. 'He fell off that bike on purpose, as soon as he heard the old boy shout.'

'You told us,' Travis said.

'And I almost got caught myself trying to help him. But he wouldn't get up; just lay on the ground snivelling.'

Travis nodded. 'He'll be snivelling some more by the time we're finished with him. We've only just started.'

'Nice of him to leave his shed unlocked so that we could get his bike, wasn't it, T?' Jackie said. 'I mean ... Travis.'

'It was,' Travis snarled. 'And remind me to tell him that it's laying at the bottom of the river.'

The three boys laughed.

'So, what do we do next?' Craig asked.

Travis stared across the road to the house they had just watched Rory enter. 'We wait for our friend to come out,' he said. 'He can't stay in there for ever.'

'Have another slice of birthday cake, Rory,' Donny's mum said. 'There's plenty left.'

Rory glanced at Donny, who was grinning.

'What are you smirking at, Donny Douglas?' his mum asked. 'Don't you like the cake? And I made it specially, too.'

'I love it Mum, really. And Rory does, too, don't you?'

Rory nodded enthusiastically. 'Nearly as good as the cakes my mum makes – and she's a fantastic cook.'

Mrs Douglas raised her eyebrows and smiled. 'That was a compliment, right?'

Rory wasn't certain what he was meant to answer, but he nodded. 'Oh, definitely.'

Mrs Douglas laughed. 'Good answer. We'll get along fine.'

Donny's parents were every bit as nice as their son had said they were, but after a couple of hours in the house, both boys were itching to get out on their bikes.

Mr Douglas seemed to notice his son gazing towards the large window overlooking the front garden. 'Are we keeping you, Donny?' he said. 'Or are you waiting for someone else to arrive?'

'I just thought that me and Rory might go for a ride,' Donny said.

'Now there's a surprise,' Mr Douglas answered. 'Go on, then. And keep an eye on him, Rory. Don't let him go too fast on that new machine of his.'

'Oh, I won't,' Rory answered, getting to his feet. 'And I just … well…' He felt his face reddening. 'I wanted to thank you both for letting Donny give me his old BMX. My mum said that I should write a proper thank-you letter, and I will. But it might take a while. I'm not great at letter-writing.'

'Neither is Donny,' Mrs Douglas replied. 'But we're very glad that you're having the bike. Enjoy yourselves.'

Rory and Donny needed no further encouragement. They both shot from the room.

'And be careful out there!' Mrs Douglas called after them.

'Here they come, lads.'

Travis and his two friends retreated into the cover of the large, bushy shrubs. They were completely hidden from view as Rory and Donny rode by.

'That's a fantastic new BMX his friend's got,' Travis said. 'Top of the range. And the one Rory's riding isn't bad, either.'

'Doesn't seem right that Rory should get another bike so soon after losing his old one, does it, T?' Craig said. 'He doesn't deserve it after what he's done.'

Travis nodded. 'We'll trail them and see where they're going.'

The three boys waited for a few moments more, giving Rory and Donny a head start. And then they followed on their bikes.

Up ahead, Rory and Donny had no idea that they were being tracked. They were simply enjoying getting used to their new machines. They rode away from the quiet housing area and headed into the old part of the city, steadily climbing towards the area around Edinburgh Castle.

Travis, Craig and Jackie followed, never getting too close but never letting the two unsuspecting boys out of their sight.

Eventually, close to the castle, they watched the two younger bikers come to a halt by an ice-cream van that was parked on one side of the cobbled street.

They saw Rory get off his BMX, give it to Donny to hold, and then delve into a pocket as he walked towards the van.

'Oh, isn't that nice,' Travis said. 'He's buying his friend an ice cream. So, here's the plan, lads.' He got off his bike and passed it to Jackie.

'What's going on?' Jackie asked nervously.

'Watch and learn,' Travis smirked.

'But what are you going to do?' Craig said.

Travis smiled. 'I'm going to get myself a new bike,' he growled. 'I'll teach young Rory that's it not a good idea to upset me, and I'll teach his friend that it's an even worse idea to be Rory's mate.'

'And what do you want us to do?'

'Nothing,' Travis said. 'This one's down to me. Just take my bike to the park. I'll meet you there later, with a new machine.'

Craig looked worried. 'You should let one of us come with you, T. Just in case something goes wrong.'

'Don't tell me what to do, Craig,' Travis snarled. 'You think I can't get a bike away from those two up there?'

'No, but—'

'Then do what I say.'

Craig shrugged his shoulders and then nodded obediently.

'I'll see you both later,' Travis said and started walking slowly towards the ice-cream van.

And then, he started to run.

Twenty

Travis arrived like an explosion. Ice cream flew through the air, both bikes crashed to the ground and Rory and Donny were sent sprawling onto the cobbles.

Walkers and sightseers stared open-mouthed as the older boy loomed over the two youngsters, eyes wild and fists clenched. He glared down at Rory.

'How's that, Rory?' Travis bawled. 'Teach you, eh? You ever grass on me again and you'll end up in the river, like your bike.'

He spun around to Donny, who had landed face first on the cobbles and was clutching one shoulder as blood streamed from his nose. 'And you, whoever you are, don't hang around with Rory. It's not good for your health.'

He leaned down and yanked Donny's brand new BMX from the ground. 'Nice this,' he said, eyes blazing. 'Think I'll take it for a little ride.'

Before anyone could stop him, Travis was on the bike and pedalling away.

'Stop!' Donny managed to shout. 'No! Stop him, someone! Please!'

Rory's head was spinning, but he clambered unsteadily to his feet and picked up his bike.

'I'll get him,' he said fiercely.

'Not you, Rory!' Donny called. 'He's too— Don't!'

But Rory wasn't listening; he was already racing away over the cobbles, desperate to keep Travis in sight.

'Rory!' Donny yelled again. He staggered to his feet, still clutching his shoulder as a woman came running over.

'Let me help you,' she said.

Donny flinched, as a stab of pain shot through his arm and up into his neck. 'My shoulder,' he gasped. 'I think it's broken.'

'We saw everything,' the woman said. 'My husband's phoned the police. He's speaking to them right now.'

Rory stood up on his pedals as he flew downhill over the bumpy cobbles at breakneck speed. He was already gaining on Travis.

Up ahead, Travis was grinning as he rode. He had enjoyed every second of the attack, although he would have preferred to stay longer. But there had been too many people around. Travis had banked on any onlookers being surprised by the speed of his assault and too shocked to intervene. And that was exactly how it had worked out.

He'd had his revenge and as a bonus he had a brand new, top-of-the-range BMX to sell on. He laughed aloud and then glanced back to make sure he wasn't being followed.

But he was.

It was Rory. He was a long way back, but gaining rapidly.

'Ha!' Travis muttered to himself. 'You want to play, Rory? Game on!'

He swerved off the cobbles into a narrow side street, still heading downhill and picking up speed. Travis knew these streets like the back of his hand. And he also knew that he couldn't beat his young pursuer for speed. But that wasn't the idea. He was going to take Rory on a rough ride … into danger.

Travis slowed as he came to a small gap between the roadside buildings. He turned into it and peered down a long descent of steep stone steps. At one edge of the steps was a narrow rainwater gully no more than twenty centimetres wide. He had ridden down here many times with other members of the gang; he used the terrifying descent as a test of their bravery. The only way to reach the bottom safely was to go carefully but quickly down the gully. Trying to ride down the steps meant a certain crash and a terrifying fall.

Travis glanced back, making sure that Rory had seen him, and then started downward. He couldn't look back again, it was too risky. But as he rode swiftly down at a frightening angle, eyes glued to the gully, he listened all the while for the sound of his pursuer crashing onto the cold, hard stone.

Rory had never been this way before. He turned into the narrow gap and paused as he spotted the steps dropping steeply away. Then he saw the gully and knew instantly that it was the only way down.

Bravely, Rory plunged downwards into the darkness, his face a mask of concentration, his eyes glued to the centre of the narrow gully. It was far too dangerous to use the pedals, so he freewheeled, his hand lightly feathering the brake as he sped lower and lower. The gully was damp with rainwater, glistening black and slippery.

Once, as he applied a little too much pressure to the brake, a wheel slipped and he moved horribly close to the edge of the steps. But he eased the brake, straightened and his nerve-tingling descent continued.

When he reached the bottom of the gully and emerged into daylight, Rory saw Travis pedalling away and realized that he had actually made up ground on the gang leader.

Travis skidded around a corner, almost broadsiding into a busier street. The pavements were packed with pedestrians who stopped and stared as the boy on the BMX flipped the machine from road to pavement and back to the road again.

'Hey!' someone shouted angrily. 'You idiot!'

Rory went zooming by, neatly and skilfully avoiding more pedestrians who had stopped to see what all the fuss was about.

'And there goes another one!' a man yelled.

Unseen by either of the boys, they had passed a side turning where a police car was parked. And as the BMX bikes raced onwards, the car's engine started and the vehicle moved out to follow.

Travis was growing tired of this game. He dearly wanted to stop and thump Rory. But he couldn't do that on a busy street, especially as he was on a stolen bike. It was all too risky. A passer-by might intervene and help the smaller boy. And Travis couldn't take that chance. He pedalled on until he reached another turning, and realised instantly how he could gain the advantange he needed. 'Come on, Rory!' he yelled. He took the sharp turn to the right, knowing that Rory was still gaining. But that was exactly what Travis had in mind.

As Rory took the same turn he found himself laughing aloud. This was like a berm on a BMX course, only easier.

They tore onward into what was familiar territory for Travis. The road was quiet, narrow and empty of pedestrians. Best of all, as far as Travis was concerned, it was also a dead end.

Up ahead was a small, circular pebbled area, surrounded by a few trees. It was almost like an arena – the perfect place to deal with Rory once and for all.

Travis pedalled hard and then braked hard, turning the BMX side on so that he was directly in Rory's path. He grinned as the young boy came rocketing towards him, waiting for him to stop.

But Rory didn't stop. He had made his decision.

He waited until he was less than five metres from the other boy and then, without slowing, he wrenched the handlebars of his BMX to the left and went sliding, broadside, towards Travis, his left foot dragging over the ground for support, right leg raised up.

Rory skidded in, rubber burning and gravel spitting into the air. He saw Travis's eyes go wide with alarm as he realized there was no time to get out of the way.

The moment of impact was perfect. Rory jabbed his right leg forward and it struck Travis heavily in the side, sending him sprawling.

Rory crashed to the ground, too, but he didn't care.

He'd got in the first, heavy blow. Travis was writhing on the ground like a fish out of water, gasping for air, all the breath knocked from his body.

Rory leapt up, fists clenched and ready to carry on the battle.

Then he heard the siren and turned to see a police car come to a halt.

The two police officers jumped out and came running over.

'Right, you two, that's it,' one of them yelled. 'Race over!'

Rory smiled. The race *was* over, and he had won.

Twenty-one

The police officers had received a radio message concerning a serious assault and a bike theft from an area close to the castle. They had spotted for themselves two boys on BMX bikes hurtling away from that part of the city. They had even been given a vague description of one of the boys involved, and Travis fitted that description. It looked as though they had caught the main culprit and his partner in crime.

The bikes were loaded into the back of the vehicle and the two boys ushered into the rear seats.

As the car pulled away, Travis spoke first. 'It wasn't me who took the bike,' he said to the officers. 'It was this kid. I don't even know him.'

'That's not true,' Rory said defiantly. 'His name's Travis.'

'He took the bike and I rode after him,' Travis went on quickly, this time with a hint of panic in his voice. 'I was trying to stop him.'

The police officer in the passenger seat looked

back. 'Aye, sure you were,' he said. 'You're a really good citizen aren't you? Well, save your breath for now. We'll sort it when we get to the station.'

Travis glared threateningly at Rory, as if daring him to reveal what had really happened.

But Rory wasn't scared of Travis any more. 'You're just a bully and a coward,' he said. 'You're pathetic.'

Travis clenched his fists and glared furiously at the boy at his side but the police officer turned back again. 'Leave it!' he growled.

Rory's thoughts had turned to Donny. 'Do you know what happened to my friend?' he asked the officer.

'Friend?' the policeman said, glancing back again. 'Someone's been taken to hospital after an assault, that's all we've heard on the radio. I don't know how he is.'

'I didn't do it. It was him!' Travis yelled. 'You can't get me for assault because I didn't do a thing except try to help.'

'Save it, lads,' the police officer said. 'You'll get your chance to explain soon enough.'

The vehicle cruised through the city streets and was soon pulling in to the police station car park.

Rory and Travis were led through double doors into the reception area. As they walked in, a man and woman sitting there turned to look at them.

The woman stood up and pointed at Travis. 'That's him,' she said loudly. 'That's the bully who attacked those poor boys and stole the bike.' She turned to Rory and smiled. 'And that's the young lad who tried to stop him.'

Rory was getting another ride in a police car, but this time his mum was sitting next to him in the rear seats.

'I nearly fainted when the police called,' Mary said.

'I'm sorry, Mum,' Rory said.

'Picking you up from the police station is getting to be a habit.'

'Yeah, I know and I'm really sorry.'

'And what are the neighbours going to say when they see us arrive home in this?'

Rory shrugged. 'They're used to police cars outside our house.'

Mary frowned, but then she smiled. 'I'm proud of you,' she said to Rory as they neared their home. 'It was very brave, but a bit reckless. You could have been hurt.'

'Donny has been hurt.'

'Yes, poor boy,' Mary answered. 'The policeman said he'd heard from the hospital that he's got a broken shoulder.'

'Can I go and visit him later?'

'Of course. I'll call his parents and we'll both go. He's got to stay in hospital overnight, just to make sure he's okay after the bang on the head.'

'At least the police have got Travis,' Rory said.

Mary nodded. 'That boy is big trouble. I saw him as I came in. Being led away in tears – shouting, claiming it wasn't him, putting the blame on everyone but himself. I don't think you'll being seeing him for a while, or the rest of his gang.'

The car turned into their street and the police offer who was driving suddenly gestured towards their house. 'We've got company,' he said. 'No one mentioned this to me.'

Rory and Mary stared through the windscreen at yet another police car. And it was parked outside their house.

'What's going on?' Mary said.

'Don't know,' the policeman said. 'Let's go and find out, eh?' He stopped the car and they got out.

But before they even reached the house, the front door opened and two more police officers appeared with Rory's dad following them.

'Eddie?' Mary said quickly.

Eddie looked towards his wife and shrugged his shoulders. 'They say I broke into a house and stole some money,' he said innocently. 'Would *I* do that? I told them, I'm a changed man.'

'Oh, Eddie.'

Grace appeared in the doorway and stood with her mum and brother as they watched Eddie being driven away.

Brother and sister looked anxiously at their mum, but this time there were no tears.

Mary simply sighed as the vehicle turned the corner and disappeared. 'Let's go inside,' she said to her two children.

Twenty-two

TWO MONTHS LATER

Okay, riders, let's set 'em up!

The eight competitors in the final rode onto the starting gate and manoeuvred their bikes into position. There were just a few tense moments to go before the race began. The BMX arena was packed and excited spectators lined the course.

Rory glanced down the track, knowing that his life had been like a BMX race over the past few incredible months. The explosive start, the twists and turns, the humps and bumps, the frantic fight to the finish.

A BMX race was a bumpy, bruising ride, but Rory had survived just about the roughest ride imaginable. So this race – the most important of his career so far – was nothing to fear. He was nervous, but not scared. He was determined to do well and to win, but he wasn't afraid of failure.

Riders ready!

The boys edged forward, the front wheels of their bikes just resting against the metal gate.

Rory's family and friends were there at the trackside, ready to cheer him on, every one of them delighted at the way the sport had made such a huge difference to his life.

As far as Rory was concerned, this race was for them all, to thank them for the way they had stuck by him. He wanted to make them proud. Most of all, Rory wanted to do well for Donny, who had hoped to be there in the final, battling against his great mate, but was still sidelined by the shoulder injury.

'Go, Rory!'

Rory heard Donny's shout and smiled.

Watch the gate!

This was it.

The crowd was hushed. Everyone – riders and spectators at the trackside – silently counted down the beeps.

Then the gate crashed down, eight BMX bikes leapt forward and every single person in the crowd yelled for their favourite.

Rory was in lane three, and as eight bikes raced towards the berm side by side, he found himself in the middle of the pack.

These were top riders. Each one had fought to reach this final and each one was battling for victory.

No one was giving any ground as they reached the berm and leaned into the bend, so tightly bunched that they looked like one seething mass of wheels in motion.

There was no clear leader as the pack emerged from the berm. Any one of four bikes might have been in front, and the four remaining riders were just a whisper behind.

They reached the bump and went bunny-hopping over, both wheels off the ground. Now the jostling for position really began.

Rory drove at the pedals, realizing that he was in second place.

'Come on, son!' Mary shouted.

'Go, Rory, go!' Grace yelled.

He was flying now, bunny-hopping again and landing right alongside the leader. As they hurtled towards the next turn he snatched the best riding line. And this time, when the bikes emerged from the corner, there was no doubt about who was at the front – Rory.

'Wow, look at him go!' Phil yelled. 'Amazing!'

'I told you!' Richard Vaughton shouted, already applauding. 'I told everyone. That boy is going to be a champion.'

Rory was all power now, surging further ahead with each turn of the pedals. There was a clear bike's length between him and the rider in second place at the last turn, and down the final straight he increased his lead even more.

Rory crossed the line with cheers ringing in his ears. He skidded to a standstill and pulled off his helmet, just in time to hear the announcement.

'The winner is number three, *Rory Temu!*'

Rory threw his head back, stared up at the sky and yelled. 'Yeeeessss!

He was a champion for the very first time.

Rory sat on his bed and glanced at the winner's medal resting on the duvet. He smiled as he relived the final in his mind, riding the race from start to finish. It had been unbelievable. And he knew that today's victory was just the beginning of his quest to get to the very top as a BMX rider.

On the bedroom wall was a large poster of the London 2012 Olympic site, with a fantastic view of the brand new BMX track. Rory stared at the poster. He wouldn't be racing there at London 2012, but he would be there watching, thanks to Grace and Mr Vaughton. Unknown to Rory, Grace had suggested to the teacher that he apply for tickets online and the fantastic news was that his application had been successful.

Rory was going to the Games, this time as a spectator. But he knew for certain that he would race over the same course one day. And he would win. He knew it now. He was a winner.

After that came the Olympic Games of 2016. He was going to be there. And this wasn't just a dream – it was possible. Anything was possible if you wanted it enough. Rory had realized that too, now.

Rory reached under the bed and pulled out his secret tin. He'd just completed a new list that he wanted to put in the tin for safekeeping. It was called the 'Things I must do …' and things I must NOT' list. 'Do the washing up more often' almost made it into the bottom three, but Rory was only really interested in number one.

This time he read the list in reverse order.

10. RUN A MARATHON.

9. EAT CAULIFLOWER CHEESE.

8. PLAY THE BAGPIPES.

7. Do the washing up more often.

6. Get to school on time.

5. Go to the gym to build up my muscles.

4. Climb Ben Nevis.

3. Get some decent racing gear.

2. Buy Grace a new computer.

1. Win a BMX Gold Medal at the Rio 2016 Games!

Official London 2012 novels
Collect the series

Parallel lines

Blessed with twin talents, Sam Warder appears to have it all. A lightning-fast scrum-half on the rugby pitch, he also performs feats of strength and agility on the parallel bars. But the London 2012 Games are approaching and Sam is at a crossroads. Flying in the face of peer pressure, he chooses Gymnastics as his sport. And then the threatening text messages begin... Can Sam hold fast to his Olympic odyssey in a school where rugby is a religion?

ISBN 978-1-84732-750-5 • £5.99

Running in her shadow

A gifted track and field athlete, Megan Morgan has all the makings of an Olympic superstar. Whether sprinting, jumping or hurdling, her body moves like quicksilver and her sporting dreams look set to become reality. Backing Megan all the way is her determined mother. A promising athlete in her youth, she will not rest until her daughter competes for Team GB. But where is the line between love and obsession? And how much pressure can Megan withstand?

ISBN 978-1-84732-763-5 • £5.99

Wheels of fire

Rory Temu is unstoppable on his battered BMX. Weaving and dodging though the Edinburgh streets, there's no obstacle he won't tackle. Such brilliance on a bike could take Rory far – maybe even as far as the Olympic Games. But a gang on the streets has been watching closely, and the members have their own plans for Rory's talents. Rory has a gift and he intends to use it, but can he keep his balance over such rough terrain?

ISBN 978-1-84732-813-7 • £5.99

Deep waters

Lucy Chambers lives to swim. Tipped as a potential Paralympian, she has watched the Aquatics Centre rise up near her London home and hopes to make a real impression there in 2012. But the ripples of Lucy's success have reached her mother, Sarah, who left her soon after she was born. Both mother and daughter share a passion for swimming – but is now the right time to start sharing in each other's lives? For Lucy, the waters have never been deeper...

ISBN 978-1-84732-764-2 • £5.99